Todd's de... hint
of a dim... ed,
his eyes ... t
impish way.

She rose and slid the chair beneath the table. "I need to give this whole idea some thought. I'd always hoped my partner would be a friend, someone I've already established a relationship with, someone I can trust. Not a perfect stranger."

His face brightened like the sun. "You have that half-right." He rose and moved to her side.

She squinted at him. "Half-right?"

"Perfect is correct. I am that. But a stranger?" No. Your nephew stole my laptop. You know me well."

Jenni struggled to hold her grin at bay.

"And as for friendship," he continued, "only time will tell. You never know what the future may bring."

Books by Gail Gaymer Martin

Steeple Hill Books

The Christmas Kite

Love Inspired

Upon a Midnight Clear #117
Secrets of the Heart #147
A Love for Safekeeping #161
**Loving Treasures* #177
**Loving Hearts* #199
Easter Blessings #202
  "The Butterfly Garden"
The Harvest #223
  "All Good Gifts"
**Loving Ways* #231
**Loving Care* #239
Adam's Promise #259
**Loving Promises* #291
**Loving Feelings* #303

*Loving

GAIL GAYMER MARTIN

enjoys a busy life—writing, traveling and singing God's praises. She lives with her amazingly wonderful husband in Lathrup Village, Michigan. Gail praises God for the gift of writing and a career she never dreamed possible. She is multipublished in nonfiction and has written over thirty works of fiction.

Her novels have been finalists for numerous awards and have won the Holt Medallion 2001 and 2003, the Texas Winter Rose 2003, the American Christian Romance Writers 2002 Book of the Year Award and *Romantic Times* Reviewers Choice Best Love Inspired novel of 2002 with *A Love for Safekeeping*. Gail loves to hear from her readers. Write to her at P.O. Box 760063, Lathrup Village, MI, 48076 or visit her Web site at www.gailmartin.com.

LOVING FEELINGS

GAIL GAYMER MARTIN

Published by Steeple Hill Books™

STEEPLE HILL BOOKS

ISBN 0-373-87313-1

LOVING FEELINGS

This edition published by arrangement with Steeple Hill Books.

www.SteepleHill.com

Printed in U.S.A.

Your beauty should not come from outward adornment, instead, it should be that of your inner self, the unfading beauty of a gentle and quiet spirit, which is of great worth in God's sight.

—*1 Peter* 3:3–4

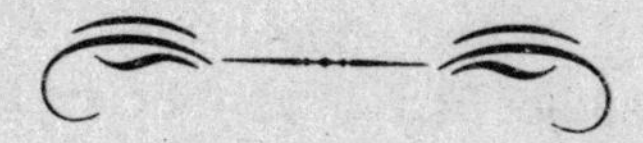

For all women who have survived breast cancer,
I wish you God's blessings.
Thank you to so many who've shared
their real-life stories:
Authors Molly Noble Bull and Joyce Livingston;
to Robin Heath for sharing her heartfelt journey;
thanks to reader Deb Luurs for sharing
her wedding story.
To author Flavia Crowner and Heidi
at the Gilette Visitors Center in Grand Haven
for setting information.

Chapter One

Chi-ching. Rat-ta-tat. Chi-ching. Thwang.

Jenni Anderson paused and listened. The muffled noise buffeted down the hallway. Cory. What was he doing? She moved closer to his doorway and pressed her ear against the wood.

Chi-ching. Whirr. Rat-ta-tat. Bah-ding.

She pulled her head away and rapped her knuckles against the door. Though he was only eight, she had always tried to respect his privacy. "Cory, what are you doing?"

The racket stopped.

"Nothing." His tone reflected his irritation.

"Can I come in?" Jenni asked, placing her hand on the knob and containing the desire to tell him to watch his mouth, but she wanted inside without a fight.

"Why?"

"Because I want to know what you're doing."

She heard his footsteps pound across the bedroom floor, and the knob turned beneath her hand. She pulled it away as the door opened an inch, and Cory peeked out through the chink. "I'm playing."

Jenni tried to peer into the room but the angle only yielded her a look at the bedroom closet door. "Playing what?"

He hesitated until guilt broke through his stoic look, and he gave in. "Pinball."

She sent her mind back to his handheld electronic games. Jenni didn't recall a pinball game that made that kind of noise. "Let me see."

She grasped the door and pushed it forward, feeling resistance until he relinquished and stepped back.

A laptop computer sat on his desk where his homework had been pushed aside. Her heart thumped as she sought a reasonable explanation. She was certain laptops weren't loaned out by Cory's school so she grasped for another possibility. She moved closer. Top brand. Looked new. "Where did you get the laptop?"

He shrugged.

"You must know where you got it, Cory."

He lifted his hooded eyes. "I found it."

"Found it?" Her heart slid to her stomach and twisted into a restricting knot. He'd found a bicycle once that belonged to a boy on the next block. After investigating, she learned he'd *found* it in the family's garage.

Jenni sank to the corner of his bed. "Where did you find it, Cory?"

"On the way home from school."

Her fortitude crumbled as she looked at his direct, unblinking gaze. "Where on the way home?"

With her persistence, his head drooped. "On the street."

"That's strange," Jenni said, rising and shifting to the computer. She moved the mouse and studied the programs, then opened a word processing program. When she hit "File" on the menu bar, the cursor sprawled down a list of documents, and she noticed one recently opened: Résumé.

She gave a click, opened the file and scanned the information. Todd Bronski. Grant Street. Loving, Michigan. Age thirty-five. Jenni let her gaze travel down the résumé. Experienced in promotion and marketing. Cory stood beside her, saying nothing.

Ashamed that she was reading a stranger's personal information, she stopped and shifted her gaze to the top of the page. "Hand me a piece of paper, please. I've found the man's telephone number."

Cory winced, and the truth settled over her like a brick. He shuffled through his homework and handed Jenni a ragged corner of looseleaf. She found a pencil and jotted down the number, then glanced at her watch. Eight o'clock in the evening. Not too late. "We'd better call Mr. Bronski. He'll be happy to know you found his computer."

Cory shoved his hands into his pockets with a frown.

Jenni turned her attention to the computer, closing the programs and turning off the power. "Put this back in the case, Cory, then bring it into the kitchen."

"We're not taking it back tonight, are we?" Cory looked at her with questioning eyes.

"Probably not."

"Then I don't know why I can't play pinball for a while."

"It doesn't belong to you, Cory. Please put the computer into the case like I asked."

She spun around and forced herself down the hallway, wanting to shake him with his impudence. He stole it from somewhere, she was sure. Emotions reeled through her, feelings of hopelessness and failure she'd felt so often with Cory's mounting bad behavior. Jenni tried to remember when it began. The past couple of years, she speculated. It had happened gradually.

Jenni sank into a kitchen chair and waited, trying to decide how to handle the situation. If she challenged Cory now without the facts, she'd end up arguing with him. If she didn't say anything, she'd be condoning what he did.

Cory finally appeared in the doorway, lugging the laptop in its black zippered case. He plopped it on the kitchen table and sank into a chair, his arms folded across his chest. "I never have any fun," he grumbled.

"Sorry." *Neither do I,* she thought, as her problems flooded over her and she drowned in their wake.

"What can I do?" he asked.

"Your homework, after I call the owner of the computer."

Cory lowered his hands to the table and cupped his chin against them, his eyes downcast.

Jenni carried the scribbled number to the telephone and punched the buttons, trying to decide what to say. After the fourth ring, she shifted to hang up the phone, but the ringing stopped, replaced by a pleasant masculine voice.

She took a deep breath. "Sorry to disturb you, but my name is Jenni Anderson. I'm looking for Todd Bronski?"

"This is Todd."

She could hear the hesitation in his voice. "I'm calling about your computer. Your laptop."

The line went silent for a moment. "What?" he said finally.

"I believe you're missing a laptop computer."

"Can't be. I left it in my car."

"You may have, but right now it's in my house. My eight-year-old said he found it."

"Found it? An eight-year-old? I don't think so."

Jenni swallowed. "I wouldn't think so, either, Mr.

Bronski, but it's here nonetheless. I'm sorry." She knew he was bewildered by the tone of his voice. "It's late, I know, so could we return it to you tomorrow?"

"My laptop?" He mumbled into the phone. "Are you sure?"

"Yes. I—I found your résumé."

Silence filled the line.

"I'll drop it off tomorrow, if that's okay. Around three."

For assurance, Jenni gave him her address and telephone number, then disconnected and peered at Cory. What could she do? He'd gotten into one thing after another. The school counselor, even the social worker, had talked to him at school. He was a disturbed child, and even prayer hadn't made a difference.

Sometimes she wondered why she had bothered to pray. She'd wasted so many hours with useless pleading, but the Lord hadn't seemed to listen. Since her mother died of breast cancer just before she graduated from high school, Jenni's life had been heading on a downward spiral.

She'd thought her mother's death had been the worst experience of her life until Jenni had also been diagnosed with breast cancer. The horror of it ripped her spirit. She'd been in her late twenties—too young, she'd thought—but she hadn't been too young. Within weeks, she'd gone through surgery, and then another blow occurred during Jenni's chemotherapy treatments when her sister died. The memories left her aching.

She turned off her self-pity and focused on Cory. "It's time we talk."

"You said I have to do my homework."

"I know, and you will after we talk."

Jenni clamped her jaw, holding back her irritation as she waited for Cory in her car after school. He'd gotten into trouble and had to sit in the principal's office again. Amid her frustration lay guilt. What had she done wrong?

So often when she lay in bed at night, feeling alone and forsaken, she asked God to give her strength and to help her be a good role model for Cory since she had to raise him alone. She'd taken him to Sunday school and church. They prayed together, and he knew about Jesus, but he didn't seem to connect that God loved him just as Jenni did.

Jenni turned off her internal struggle and peered at the school's entrance. Cory finally appeared, plodding down the sidewalk, kicking at stones. When he opened the car door, he slipped in without a word.

"We've kept Mr. Bronski waiting, Cory. I told him we'd be there around three o'clock."

"Wasn't my fault," the boy muttered, his fists clenched against his legs as if he were heading for the guillotine.

"You got into trouble at school so it *was* your fault. Sometimes, Cory, we make mistakes, and we have to live up to them and admit them. Then we try to do better next time."

He turned his mottled face toward her. "You always believe *them.* I didn't do *anything!*"

Jenni held back her response. She wouldn't argue with the boy. She'd made that mistake, and she became as immature as he was. He had an excuse as an eight-year-old. She was thirty-three.

Thirty-three going on seventy. That's how she felt sometimes. She drew up her shoulders, forcing away the negative feelings, and looked for something positive. Despite her setbacks, she'd taken her small dream and made it a lucrative and successful reality.

Owning her own business had been her plan since she could remember. Jenni had a knack for making sweets—pies, cakes and cookies—but one day she stumbled on an idea for candy and that day made all the difference.

Her homemade-candy business had been so successful, she had eventually quit her secretarial position and spent more time at home with Cory. Her basement had become her cooking studio where she'd created unique chocolate confections.

The past months had helped her to realize she needed a real candy store, a place to display her luscious treats. Selling from her home had worked until her chocolate concoctions had gotten too popular.

Jenni slowed and looked for the Grant Street address. Finally she saw the number she was looking for on the front of what appeared to have been an old farmhouse. She eased to the curb and parked. "This is it," she said to Cory.

He hunched down as if wanting to vanish into the upholstery. "You go. I'll wait here," he muttered.

"No, you won't." She opened the door, reached behind the seat and pulled out the laptop. "You need to explain where you found the computer."

When she reached the passenger side, Cory had made no move to open his door. She prayed he hadn't locked it. He did that sometimes. When she pushed on the handle, the door opened and Cory grudgingly climbed out.

The house looked well-kept with white painted siding and gray shutters. A few spring flowers pushed their green stems through the moist earth, hinting that warmer days were around the corner. A long porch stretched across the front, and Jenni climbed the steps, then paused for Cory to join her. When he stomped up behind her, she rang the bell.

Waiting, she took deep breaths to calm her inner turmoil. Cory was her responsibility, and what he did reflected on her character. She'd always been an honest person, and his sinful behavior had lain against her heart since he'd begun to lie. She'd tried everything. Nothing made a difference, and the situation seemed to be getting worse.

There was a noise from inside, and when the door swung open, Jenni faced a medium-built man dressed in a well-fitted business suit. "I'm Jenni Anderson, and this is Cory." She shifted him forward. "He's the one who found your computer."

He scowled, peering first at her, then Cory. "You're late." His focus drifted downward to the laptop clutched in Jenni's grasp.

"I'm sorry," Jenni said. "Cory got into a... We were delayed. I hope we didn't keep you waiting."

"I have an interview, and it's—" he glanced at his watch "—nearly four. I can't invite you in."

Jenni wavered, wanting to learn more about the computer and how Cory got his hands on it, but she couldn't delay the man. She felt the weight of the computer in her grasp and lifted it toward him. "Here's your laptop."

He stared at it a moment before taking it. "That's mine all right. I—I'm sorry. I'm in a rush." He shifted and leaned inside the house, exchanging the laptop for an attaché case. "Look, I have your address. Could I stop by later or call you? The situation needs some explaining."

"It does," she said, noticing he'd shifted his attention to Cory while his gaze softened. When he focused on Jenni, he looked distracted and stepped forward. "I really need to get moving."

Jenni backed away, tripping over Cory's foot. She grabbed the boy's shoulder to keep from losing her balance, and at the same time, the man clutched her arm to stop her fall. His strong grasp relaxed as she righted herself.

"I'll talk to you later," he said, bounding down the porch steps.

"All right," she said, watching him climb into an SUV and back out of the driveway.

He gave her a fleeting wave as he pulled away.

She stood on his porch, watching him go.

Cory glanced at her, his face looking less tense than it had, and he skipped down the stairs.

The only thing Jenni felt like skipping was dinner. Her stomach was in knots.

Leaving the city hall, Todd dropped his attaché case onto the passenger seat and settled behind the wheel of his SUV. He rubbed his thumb and index finger against his eyes. Had his job interview gone well? He had no idea. The man had been unresponsive.

Maybe he'd made a mistake moving to Loving. The way Todd had looked at it, a tourist town had to have marketing positions. The place was filled with resorts, marinas, special events and unique attractions. Everyone was competing against the other, and promotion was the key.

His friend Dale Levin had encouraged the move. They'd met at Michigan State University years earlier and had remained friends even though their careers had taken them to different parts of the state. He respected Dale's opinion, and with all the drama in Todd's life, getting away from Detroit and its bad memories had seemed to make sense. Now he wondered.

Turning the key in the ignition, Todd looked in the rearview mirror, then checked the side mirror before backing out of the parking spot. Memory of the interview bounced in his head, and he wondered if he might have forgotten something or if perhaps he'd been too abrupt. Some of the man's questions had seemed demeaning. Todd wondered if he might have offended the man. *What's new, Todd, old boy? You've done that before.*

At thirty-five he felt unsettled. He hated the feeling. Life had dealt him too many blows, and he wished he could let them roll off his shoulders like rain, but he couldn't. They soaked into his being and left him saturated with regret.

Todd straightened his back and tried to focus on the present. He could do nothing about the past, except learn from it. But had he?

The light turned red just ahead, and he pressed on the brake, catching his attaché case as it slid forward. Seeing the dark case brought his laptop to mind. He slid his hand into his pocket before the light changed to green, pulled out a piece of paper and glanced at the address written on it. The Anderson residence was on his way home.

Six o'clock in the evening. His stomach twinged, reminding him that he hadn't eaten since breakfast. His thoughts about the laptop had unsettled him, and the day had trudged past, leaving his appetite unresponsive.

He wondered if he would be interrupting the family's dinner. In truth, he didn't care. The woman and her kid had certainly messed up his day, and now he wanted to get to the bottom of the computer mystery. How had an eight-year-old boy gotten his grubby little hands on his laptop?

He turned at the next block and headed down Waverly, watching the house numbers as he drove. He slowed, certain the home had to be nearby. He spotted the address and pulled into the driveway.

The small bungalow had been painted yellow with black shutters. The colors reminded him of a yellow jacket. Like the insect's sting he ached as he recalled the young boy's belligerent expression. Feelings he tried to evade rushed over him like a swarm of angry wasps.

Todd sat in the car a moment wondering if his thoughts were a premonition. Yellow jackets, wasps and stings. He shook his head to shed his growing anxiety. He almost felt sorry for the Anderson woman. She seemed at a loss, yet he sensed her defensiveness for the boy was like that of any mother. She was a pretty woman, too, and he wondered why her husband hadn't marched the boy to his door.

Or perhaps she had none. Single moms were not uncommon.

No matter, the boy needed help. The child's behavior seemed almost too familiar. Todd's thoughts flew back to his brother. Ryan, the problem child. Ryan, the teenage hoodlum. Ryan, the armed robber. The recollection weighted down his already-lagging spirit.

Pushing open the car door, Todd breathed in the damp, dusky air. Spring offered a new beginning. Soon the sun would brighten the landscape for hours longer, the air would be warmer, the sky would be bluer. Like the change of season, Todd, too, needed a change—in attitude—and he definitely needed to grasp on to a new beginning.

He closed the car door and headed up the walk. The first concrete step had crumbled at the edge, and the porch had a small crack running along the side where the ground seemed to be settling. He guessed this family worked hard to make ends meet. Todd was curious what the woman's husband did for a living. He wondered about a lot of things.

He gave the doorbell a push and waited. Soon he heard footsteps and saw the knob turn. When the door opened, the woman studied him through the storm door. A look of recognition settled on her face before she invited him inside.

As he stepped into the foyer, the scent of food surrounded him. Beef, perhaps, and something else, something sweet and rich. His stomach gave a silent growl as he backed away to let her close the door. "I'm afraid this is bad timing. I've interrupted your dinner."

"No. It's in the oven," she said. "I was expecting you."

His thoughts banged around in his head until he spit them out. "Listen, Mrs. Anderson—"

"It's Miss Anderson. Jenni."

Miss. The title surprised him. He looked into her large gray eyes. "Miss Anderson."

"Jenni," she said again.

Seeing her strained expression, his pulse skipped. "Do you have a few minutes now so we can talk?"

She hesitated, then nodded.

He shoved his hands into his pockets, wondering if they would talk standing in the small postage-stamp-size foyer.

"Come in," she said, flagging him through the doorway to the left.

He followed her into the living room and took in the cozy environment before he took the seat she had indicated. "I'm curious," he said, as he settled into the cushion, "how your boy got his hands on my laptop."

She sat, flinching with his question, but the only thing that made sense to him was the kid had stolen it.

A frown marred her wide forehead as she gazed

at him. "I don't know, either," she said. "He said he found it."

Todd's pulse skipped. "Found it? In my car, I'm afraid. That's where I'd left it."

"I thought you must be mistaken. Perhaps you set it on the ground while you gathered up packages or something. Maybe you forgot it."

"I didn't forget it."

"You mean Cory *broke into* your car?"

Todd realized that part of the situation was his fault. "It wasn't locked. I ran into the house for a minute. I was leaving again." His back stiffened, realizing she'd put him on the defensive.

"Look," he said, hearing his voice rise, "this is about the boy—"

"I know." Her arms flopped to her sides, and he sensed her defeat. She turned to him, her eyes filled with deep emotion. "Did you call the police?"

"Why would I? I didn't realize the computer was missing until you called."

Relief spread across her face, making him wonder if this wasn't the first time the boy had gotten into trouble.

"In my opinion, the boy needs to learn—"

"His name is Cory."

The comment smacked him in the chest, and he lost some of his fight. "You're Cory's mother. You need a firmer hand on him or the kid will end up in a juvenile facility before he's ten."

As he watched, her jaw tightened, and her cloudy gray eyes misted like rain. He drew back, wanting to erase his words, wanting to do something, but he was at a loss.

Her cheek quivered as she brushed a finger across her eyes.

"I'm not his mother. His mother's dead."

Chapter Two

Todd Bronski's comment had cut her to the core, but Jenni willed her tears to subside. She watched his jaw drop as he squirmed against the chair, looking as if he wanted to vanish.

"I'm sorry," he said, his voice more humble than she'd heard since they met.

"I'm Cory's aunt. I've raised him since he was three." Memories came crashing in—her sister's death, the funeral. Who else would have accepted the challenge of raising Cory? Her father wasn't willing, and the child's father wasn't interested. Though Jenni wasn't emotionally ready to raise an active toddler, she became his guardian, trusting God would give her the ability and the patience.

Todd peered at her, his lips pressed so tightly together they were bloodless.

Jenni wanted to make a hash mark in the air. For

once she'd said something that startled him. Yet part of her writhed with this truthful comment. Cory needed help, and she didn't know what more to do.

"I know Cory needs a firm hand," she said finally.

Todd looked uneasy and cleared his throat. "That's a big job. One I wouldn't want."

They gazed at each other in silence until he finally straightened in the chair and flexed his entwined fingers. "Is he here? I suppose we need to get to the bottom of this."

"Yes. He's upstairs. I'll get him." She rose and moved to the staircase and called the boy, then returned to the sofa.

They waited a moment, eyeing each other uneasily, until Cory thudded down the stairs, but when he hit the doorway and saw Todd, he stopped.

"Cory, Mr. Bronski wants to ask you about the computer," Jenni said.

"I'm doing things." He gestured toward the staircase.

"You can finish later. Come in here, please."

He hesitated until Todd rose and motioned to him. Cory's face paled, and he left the doorway and came into the room.

"Would you tell me what happened, please?" Todd asked as he returned to his seat.

Cory stood in the center of the room, his hands in his pockets, his head drooping. "I told you. I found it. That's all."

Todd shook his head and probed for more details while Cory evaded him.

Jenni had had enough. "Tell us the truth, Cory. I'm tired of this! We'll be here all night until you do."

Cory finally broke down and related that he'd seen the laptop on the passenger seat as he passed the car. He tried the door, it was unlocked and he took it.

Jenni's chest tightened, and she longed to take the boy in her arms and squeeze the lies out of him with her love, but love didn't seem to work. At least her kind of love didn't.

"So what should we do?" Jenni asked.

Todd scowled and sank deeper into the chair. "It's late. Let's think about this and decide a fair penalty." He stared at the carpet, pursing his lips and twiddling his thumbs.

Cory shrunk at the word *penalty*.

"This isn't the end of this," Todd said finally as he focused on Cory. "We need to make some decisions, but first I want to talk with your mom—aunt. I hope you'll think about what you did."

No one spoke until Cory gave Todd a direct look.

"You can't keep lying and stealing," Todd said. "It's like a spiderweb. It keeps getting bigger and bigger until you're so tangled in the web you can't move."

Cory's eyes widened as he listened.

"Think about that, okay?" Todd looked frustrated as he edged back into the chair.

"You can go upstairs now," Jenni said, breaking the tension.

The boy turned and left the room without a word.

Rigid with stress, Jenni watched him trudge toward the staircase before she fell against the cushion.

"I'm sorry to put you through this," Todd said.

She was sorry, too. The whole situation broke her heart and seemed horribly hopeless.

Todd leaned forward, clasping his hands. "I don't want to report this to the police, but he needs to make retribution in some way or he'll never learn."

Relief washed over her. "You're right. I agree." Yet she hesitated before continuing. "And thank you."

He looked puzzled.

"I mean thanks for not calling the police." The one thing for which she'd been truly grateful was his discretion at not reporting it.

"I assume this isn't the first time he's gotten into trouble."

She shook her head, unable to say the words. Jenni studied the man as he sat across from her. She wanted to dislike him. He'd burst into her home to punish her nephew, yet despite it, she appreciated his kindness. He could have easily called the police, and the problem would no longer be his, but hers.

Reality smacked her. If Cory continued along the same path, she could lose him. Not being his mother, the courts could easily take him away and put him in a facility or a foster home. Why hadn't she adopted him? The thought shattered her. Despite the problems, she loved Cory with all her heart. She was frustrated, but she couldn't forget the day the toddler moved into her house, confused and afraid. She pushed the image aside. She'd make things work. She had to.

"I'm at a loss right now what we should do," Todd said, breaking the silence. "I don't know what programs the town has for troubled kids or what—"

"That's right. You're new here." She slammed her mouth closed, realizing that was a detail she wouldn't know if she hadn't read his résumé.

"I've been in Loving for a month. My friend Dale Levin lives here and recommended I make the move."

"I don't know him." She drew her shoulders back, trying to relieve the stress. The conversation had eased, and she wished she could feel the same. "So, you just picked up and moved. I suppose that takes courage."

"Not as much as raising a three-year-old alone."

He smiled, and she smiled back, feeling a warm sensation wash over her. She'd been on edge for the past two days and forgot what a smile felt like. "What kind of work are you looking for?"

"Don't you know? You read my résumé."

His comment smacked her between the eyes. "I didn't study it. Skimmed is about all I did."

He grinned, and she realized he was teasing.

"My work's been in the area of promotion-marketing. I promoted stage shows and events in the Detroit area. The job was interesting. Sometimes exciting."

His description didn't seem to match his expression, and Jenni wondered what story lay beneath his thoughts. "Why did you leave the position?"

She'd been right. A shadow settled over his face, and she noticed his body tense.

"A quest, I suppose," he said. "Looking for a new challenge."

"Loving's a resort town. I'm sure you'll find something challenging here."

She sensed his discomfort and decided to change the subject, but he changed it for her.

"You haven't mentioned what you do for a living," he said, obviously pleased to get the focus off himself.

"I have a candy business. Jenni's Loving Kisses. Kisses isn't a copyright, if you were wondering."

"You own the business?"

His questioning tone struck her. "Don't I look capable?"

"I didn't mean that. I'm just surprised." He shifted forward and clasped his hands together as they rested between his knees. "Who does your promotion?"

"I don't need promotion. I have all the business I can handle." That wasn't totally true, but she wouldn't admit it to him. He'd begun to look too self-satisfied again.

"Where's your shop?"

Her pulse escalated with his question. "Right here."

He pointed toward the floor. "Here. In your kitchen?"

"You sound dubious. I run the business from my basement. I make all my own candy. Sometimes when it's close to a holiday—you know, Valentine's Day and Christmas—I hire extra help."

He leaned even closer as if she'd piqued his interest. "You make a livable income working from your basement?"

"I'm not rich, but I'm doing okay. I plan to expand soon."

"In what way? Get a larger stove?"

She felt herself bristle at his comment. "No." Her voice shot out louder than she'd expected, but when she noticed his grin, she relaxed. "I'm going to open a store. I'm looking for a backer, a partner of sorts. Silent partner, preferably."

"Really?"

"Yes, really." This time he didn't smile, and his attitude riffled down her back. She wanted to knock the smug look from his face.

"I wasn't suggesting that you couldn't do it," he said, apparently realizing he'd irked her. "I'm surprised with raising a child and having so many responsibilities you're able to make a living from selling candy."

"I have good clients."

"I'd like to hear more." He glanced at his watch. "But it's late."

Jenni checked her watch and was surprised how time had flown.

Todd stood. "I better head home. Hopefully, we'll get this settled, and we'll be out of each other's hair." He moved toward the doorway.

Jenni followed him, seconding his comment about getting him out of her hair. "I'd like some idea what you have in mind."

"In mind?"

"About Cory's punishment."

"You agree he needs to make retribution of some kind?"

"Well, yes, naturally, but I expect some input."

"He stole my laptop, and I believe—"

Jenni's spine stiffened. "He's eight years old!"

"And he's a thief."

She felt as if the floor fell out from under her. "I'm sure we can come up with something together that we both agree on."

Todd paused with his hand on the doorknob. "That'll work. I'll be in touch. All I know is the boy needs to learn a lesson."

"I know," she said, wishing she could tell him it was none of his business.

But it *was* his business, and she'd have to get used to it.

* * *

Todd heard a noise. His hands paused on the computer keys, and he twisted to look out the window. A car sat in the driveway. When the doorbell rang, he headed for it and felt pleasantly surprised when he saw his visitor. "Dale. Good to see you. Come on in." He moved back to allow Dale Levin, his college buddy, into the foyer.

Dale stepped inside and slid off his shoes. "It's muddy out there." He bent down and set them on the mat. "How are things? I haven't heard from you for a few days."

"I'm fine," Todd said, waiting while Dale slipped off his jacket. Todd hung it on the coat tree, then motioned him into the living room. "Can I get you anything? Coffee? Soft drink?"

"No, thanks. I was passing by and thought I'd stop. Sorry I didn't call."

Todd shook his head to tell him it didn't matter.

"Any luck with job hunting?" Dale asked.

"I've had a couple of interviews. Nothing positive yet." He looked at Dale's expression and realized what was going on. "Hey, pal, don't feel guilty. You suggested I move to Loving, but I'm a big boy. I made the decision. I'll find a job. Don't worry."

Dale's shoulders lowered, and he sank deeper into the cushion. "It so happened last night I was thinking about my friend Ian Barry who runs a resort on Lake Michigan—Bay Breeze. Maybe you've seen it? The owner is Philip Somerville who believes in promoting the place. He's added a private marina at the resort for his own boats. They're mainly for his patrons, but I think he rents them out during slower seasons. Anyway, you get my point. I thought maybe—"

Todd chuckled. "I have an interview in a couple of days with Ian Barry."

Dale grinned. "Great minds, they say."

Todd agreed and gave him the details. During the discussion, Jenni Anderson came to mind, as she had since he'd met her a few days earlier. "I had a strange encounter a couple days ago, and it's set me to thinking."

"I see that look in your eyes, Bronski. This has to do with a woman."

Todd shrugged. "Yes, I guess it does." He told Dale the story of his stolen laptop, meeting Jenni and her search for a business partner. "What do you think?"

Dale's guffaw broke the silence. "You mean you're considering investing your money with a woman whose eight-year-old kid is a thief?"

"That's another issue. Anyway, I'm just thinking. I'd need to know a lot more about the business. Look at her books. Talk about her short- and long-range plans."

"And figure out what you really have in mind," Dale added with a wink.

"I have nothing like that in mind, pal. It's too soon."

Dale quieted as if he realized he was treading on touchy ground. "Sorry. I didn't mean to make light of Tesha's death, but it's been over two years, Todd. Don't let life pass you by like I almost did."

Todd grasped at the opportunity to refocus the conversation. "Speaking of that, how are the wedding plans? It's getting close, isn't it?"

"A few more months. In fact, I gave up my place in Grand Rapids and I've moved in with Dad until after we're married."

"You're living in town now?"

"Right, and looking for a house for us. I took a few vacation days to get settled. After we're married, we'll sell Bev's place. The kids are excited about the move."

Kids. Todd had never quite understood how a woman could change Dale's heart. His friend had vowed he'd never marry. Todd had done the same after his catastrophic marriage to Tesha. He'd used bad judgment, and he'd learned his lesson. He'd never let that happen again.

Dale rose. "I should be on my way. I just wanted to mention Bay Breeze. I'll give Ian a call and tell him you're a friend of mine."

Todd grinned. "I hope that gets me brownie points and not crossed off his list."

Dale gave Todd's arm a teasing punch, then headed for the coat tree. "No fear." He slipped on his jacket and shoes, then paused. "So, getting back to your lady friend with the minithief. Are you serious about that?"

"Not serious. Just thinking. I have money to invest, and I'm looking for something different. I'm curious, I suppose."

"Well, don't jump off the pier. Wear a life jacket."

"Who's talking? Dale Levin marrying a woman with two kids. A ready-made family. Where's *your* life jacket?"

Dale pressed his hand against his chest. "Right here, buddy. The heart. She saved me from myself, really. Sometimes we need saving from ourselves. Think about it." He reached for the doorknob and gave it a turn. "Keep me posted on the job. I'll be anxious to hear what Ian has to say."

"Good seeing you," Todd said, holding the door while his friend bounded down the porch steps. He gave a wave and stood there, watching Dale back his car out of the driveway and pull away.

Sometimes we need saving from ourselves. The words bobbed in Todd's mind like a buoy. He'd spent the past years beating up himself for not saving his brother, and now he'd set sail on a new course to save Cory.

But Dale's comment wagged in Todd's head. Did Todd need to save himself from his past and his fears? If so, could he? He no longer had faith in his decisions, especially ones that concerned the heart.

Words floated into his memory—a Bible verse he'd learned as a child. *"For it is by grace you have been saved, through faith."*

Faith. His faith had sunk to the depths of the sea, and no life preserver could save him from that.

Chapter Three

Jenni looked at the clock. Cory should be home from school in another hour. Before he'd gone to bed last night, they'd had a long talk, and she prayed that her words had sunk in. She'd felt relieved when she hadn't gotten a telephone call from the principal today. That was good news. Apparently Cory had made it through the day without getting into serious trouble.

But stealing a computer was far worse than shooting spitballs or tripping a kid in the hallway. Stealing was a serious offense and a sin, and Jenni felt lost on how to deal with Cory's growing problem.

A strand of hair sneaked from beneath her head covering, and Jenni brushed it from her eyes. She lifted the leftover filling from the double boiler to let it cool. This evening she would work with the chocolate as she always did after Cory went to bed.

The job wasn't easy. Besides hiring help, she occasionally rented a church kitchen when her orders were so great she couldn't handle them alone, but Jenni prided herself on doing the whole job—from her original recipes to final wrappings. What else did she have to do other than raising Cory? And she wasn't doing a very good job of that.

As Cory filled her thoughts, Todd Bronski charged into her mind. He'd said he'd get back to her to discuss Cory's theft. She realized Todd had the right to file a police report or get some kind of recompense for Cory's behavior, but she'd already talked with Cory—while trying to capture his evasive gaze—and hoped maybe she had gotten through.

Jenni pulled the thick netting from around her hair, hung it on a hook away from the candy and headed up the basement stairs. When she reached the kitchen, she realized how exhausted she felt, and she knew she faced more hours of work later in the evening. She opened a cabinet and pulled out a container, then spooned grounds into the coffeemaker. Caffeine would give her the go-power she needed.

As she hit the start button, the telephone rang and her heart stood still. Cory's principal. They were keeping him after school. She felt it in her bones.

She grabbed the wall phone, and after she said hello, her heartbeat kicked into fast gear, hearing Todd's voice. "I was just thinking of you," she said before she could stop herself.

"You were?"

The tone of his voice assured her he'd misconstrued her meaning. "I wondered when you'd call so we could talk about the situation with Cory. I'll feel better when it's settled."

"Aah," he said, his voice softening with a new compassion. "How about now?"

"On the telephone?" His idea lifted her spirit, knowing she could avoid seeing him face-to-face. "Sure."

"No. At your place, if that's okay. I'd like to talk with Cory, too."

"Cory's still at school, but he'll be home shortly." She truly wanted to get the matter settled. She glanced down at the huge chocolate spot on her knit top and gazed lower at her faded jeans. "What time did you want to stop by?"

"Now?"

She stared at the telephone, then remembered she hadn't put on makeup or even combed her hair since morning.

"Where are you?"

He paused. "In your driveway. I'm on my cell phone. I was passing by and figured I'd give it a try."

Jenni made a wild gesture, running her fingers through her hair, yet knowing nothing would help except a shower and time. She sighed. "Okay, but give me a minute."

She hung up the telephone, and darted into her

bedroom to fling on a clean top. At least she wouldn't look like Willy Wonka in the chocolate factory. She glanced into the mirror. No time for makeup. *He'll have to take what he gets.*

She grasped a comb just as the doorbell rang. "Coming," she called, tugging the comb through her hair. She dropped it on her dresser, then hurried to the door. "Sorry. I had to finish a little project."

"No problem," he said. "I didn't give you much notice."

"True." She pushed back the door and he stepped inside. Without her invitation, Todd walked into the living room, still wearing his jacket, and sank into the same chair he'd used before.

Jenni closed the door and joined him. She sat in the same spot as before, giving her the sensation that he'd never left. Rather than his usual business suit, Todd wore a nutmeg-colored suede jacket, and the warm tone highlighted his classic features. Striking features, she admitted.

Before she realized what she'd done, she opened her mouth and spit out her thoughts. "Has anyone every told you that you look a little like George Clooney?"

His head shot upward in surprise, then a grin broke across his serious face, and he tilted back his head with a laugh, showing a generous smile of even white teeth. She couldn't take her eyes from him.

"Never heard that one," he said. "No relation."

Embarrassed by her comment on his looks, she decided to halt the chitchat. "Cory should be home in another fifteen minutes or so."

He glanced at his watch. "That's fine. We need to talk first anyway."

Jenni couldn't forget his warm laugh and his easy smile she'd just witnessed. That side of him gave her hope. When she first met him, she'd noticed a flicker of humor and that somehow made its way through his abrupt arrogance. Yet how could she blame him for his attitude? That day she'd just announced that her nephew had swiped his laptop.

The scent of fresh coffee drifted into the room, reminding her how badly she'd wanted a pick-me-up and, she figured, a genial offer couldn't hurt this temperament. "I just made coffee. Would you like some?"

"Sure." he said. "Black, please." He leaned forward and slipped off his jacket. Beneath it, he wore a royal-blue crew-neck sweater that added to his charm.

Jenni pulled her gaze away and rose. "I'll be right back."

In the kitchen, she stood a moment to organize her thoughts. Why she was entertaining this man was far from her grasp, except she hoped he'd agree to leniency. Leniency. The situation frustrated her.

Addled, she poured two mugs of coffee and doctored hers with skim milk. As she opened the refrigerator to return the carton, the back door opened and Cory dragged in. “Who’s here?”

“Mr. Bronski.” Cory’s scowl grated on her patience. “I explained last night that he’d be back to talk.”

“I don’t want to talk to him.”

“I’m sorry. That’s not a choice, but I’ll give you a break.” She retrieved the milk from the fridge and pulled a glass from the cabinet. “How about taking some milk and a couple cookies upstairs and work on your homework for a while?” She nailed him with her look. “I’m sure you have some.” She’d noticed the bulge in his backpack.

He shrugged, then headed for the cookie jar.

“I’ll talk to Mr. Bronski first, and then I’ll call you.”

Cory didn’t respond. He carried the milk and cookies into the hallway as if pleased to make his escape, then plodded up the stairs with reverberating thuds.

Releasing a sigh, Jenni grabbed the cup handles with one hand and a covered candy dish with the other. When she returned to the living room, she set the dish on the table and handed Todd one of the mugs. “Cory just came in. I told him to start his homework, and I’d call him.”

He nodded and turned his attention to the mug. “It smells good.” He drew in a breath of fragrant steam, then took a sip.

Jenni gestured to the dish she'd brought in from the kitchen. "Would you like a kiss?"

His surprised look caught her off guard, and she swallowed a chuckle.

Todd's expression shifted to one of confusion.

She lifted the ceramic dish and set the lid on the table. "A candy kiss," she added. "Remember, I make them. You sounded interested so I thought you'd like to try one."

As she thrust the container toward him, she watched a flush creep up his sturdy neck ending just below his brown eyes, the color of milk chocolate. "Try one. See what you think." She tilted her head toward the dish.

His control seemed to resurface as he eyed the chocolates. "Homemade candy." He gave her a dubious look, then removed one of the wrapped sweets, turning it over in his fingers. "These are a lot bigger than the famous brand." He unwrapped the shiny gold foil and studied the kiss before looking toward her.

"That's because they're different. I've tucked a cherry or a macadamia nut inside."

Something simmered behind his dark eyes. Perhaps curiosity. Finally he lifted the nugget of rich chocolate and took a bite.

Jenni forced her gaze from his and focused on the candy he held as a smile inched to her mouth. "That one is definitely cherry filled."

The sweet liquid trickled onto his lower lip. Deftly he reached behind him and tugged a white handkerchief from his back pocket, catching the sticky mess before it dripped on his crew-neck sweater. “Sorry.” His gaze caught hers. “I wasn’t expecting liquid in the filling.”

“It’s part of the surprise of trying a new chocolate candy. I only do that with the cherries. Please, have another. The next one might be safer.” She grinned.

He studied her a moment before reaching to take a second piece. She watched him taste the kiss, this time more carefully. A faint smile brightened his face.

“So what do you think?” she asked, gesturing to the candy.

“It’s delicious. Different. Is it Grand Marnier?”

“Grand Marnier?” Jenni’s eyes widened.

“You know, the liqueur with the orange flavor,” he said, licking the syrupy filling from the ends of his fingers.

“Liquor! No. I’d never add alcohol.”

Surprised, Todd winced at Jenni’s vehemence. “I just thought that maybe—”

“You have the right flavor,” Jenni said, her voice much softer. “It’s a clear liquid center made with a dash of orange zest and—” she whispered “—my secret ingredient.”

He figured she was trying to soften the tension and went along with the gag. “Secret ingredient?”

She nodded.

“Can you give me a hint?”

"I'll only share that with a partner...if I find one." She tilted her head in a cute, lazy way. "And soon, I hope."

"Why the rush?" She'd captured his interest with that line.

She seemed frustrated with herself that she'd said too much, but she answered anyway. "I've drawn attention to myself and the city's been pressuring me. This neighborhood is residential and not approved for a business of this size." She grasped her mug and took a sip.

Todd latched on to that piece of news while his thoughts kicked into overdrive.

"The city officials have been patient, so I don't want to push their gracious cooperation to the limit. I figure I'd better speed up my moving plans."

Though what she said definitely piqued Todd's interest, his mind kept heading back to her earlier reaction, and he wondered about her abruptness when he'd mentioned alcohol. He decided not to go there.

Her smile faded. "I suppose we need to get down to business."

She threw him off a moment until he remembered the purpose of his visit. "Cory?"

"Right." She lifted the mug and took another sip. "What idea did you come up with?"

Without warning, he felt rotten sitting in her easy chair, eating her chocolate and talking about punishing her nephew, but it was for the boy's own good.

He sorted through his suggestions before answering her. "What do you think about something like…?" Like what? Some kind of task? "Let's say community service."

"Community service? What could Cory do for the community?"

"He can work for me. Rake leaves, polish silver, help wash my car, exercise the dog."

"You have a dog?"

She looked surprised, and so did he, he guessed. "No. I have a nice fenced-in yard, though."

Jenni laughed. "You're buying a dog to give Cory something to do?"

"Not really, but I've been thinking about it." For the last minute, he admitted to himself, wondering where that idea had come from.

"I'm not sure a dog would be punishment, but I agree raking leaves and polishing silver might be."

Todd grinned. "I don't have silver, either, but—"

"You've been thinking?"

"It was just an example."

"How would we handle this?"

He hadn't given that much thought, but wheels began to spin. "Until I start a new job, Cory could come over after school, work a couple hours and then come home. Let's say for two weeks. I could even insist he do his homework there. That should be punishment enough." He sent her a grin, hoping she'd ease up.

In the back of his mind, Todd hoped the attention might rub off on the boy and help him see the error of his ways. He winced at the memory of his brother. If he'd only shown Ryan a little special attention, if he'd only taken him to a ball game or movies. Anything. But Todd had done nothing but concentrate on his own life.

"That's fine, but I'll come with him. I don't know you that well, Mr. Bronski, and—"

"Todd, please." He felt like a jerk. Obviously he was a stranger, and she'd be nuts to let him spend time with her kid. "I understand. The problem is I don't want to tie up your time with—"

"That's okay. I know I have to punish him one way or the other, but I—"

"But you don't like punishing yourself at the same time." He figured he might as well complete her sentence.

They sat in silence a moment until he felt uneasy. "Can I talk with Cory now?"

"I'll call him down," she said, getting up.

"I'd like to talk with him privately. You know, man-to-man. He might not be as defensive if you're not around."

She flashed him an irritated look. "That's fine. I'll be in the kitchen." She walked to the staircase and gave a call.

In a few moments, Cory thumped down the stairs like a man heading for the gas chamber. Jenni steered him toward the living room, and she vanished down the hallway.

Todd shifted to the sofa and motioned for the boy to join him. He stood in the doorway, not budging. Todd patted the cushion. "You might as well sit. This will take a while."

Grudgingly, the boy tromped across the room and plopped on the far end of the sofa. He looked away from Todd, who realized he'd bitten off more than he cared to chew. He didn't say anything and sat in silence.

Time passed, and the boy grew restless.

Todd glanced at Jenni in the doorway, but when she saw the scene, she backed away, unnoticed by Cory.

The boy shifted and folded his arms.

"I had a younger brother," Todd said. "You remind me of him."

For a moment, Todd thought the boy would continue to ignore him, but to his amazement, the boy eased around to face him. "How old is he?"

"He was seventeen when he died."

"Died?" Cory's insolent expression sank to a frown. "How?"

"He got into some trouble."

The boy studied him. "What kind of trouble?"

"Big trouble." He hesitated telling the boy but decided to finish what he started. "Stealing."

For the first time, he saw the boy react. "It's time for us to talk about you, Cory."

Chapter Four

Jenni stood in the kitchen, longing to know what was happening. When she'd looked in earlier, Cory was just sitting on the far end of the sofa with one of his unpleasant looks that broke her heart. He looked so much like his mother had when she'd been angry or frustrated.

Voices drifted in from the living room while curiosity got the better of Jenni. She eased toward the doorway, listening to the muffled voices, trying to catch words and phrases. When the voices stopped and she heard rustling, she backed away from the door and opened the pantry as if involved in dinner preparation.

Cory walked into the kitchen first, his head hanging but a look of acceptance on his face. "He's making me work for him," he said with a blend of self-pity, yet with a hint of pride.

Hearing the paradoxical response, Jenni sensed that underneath his punishment, Cory needed to feel useful. Perhaps that's where she'd failed. She'd overprotected him and, in the process, gave him no sense of purpose. Or did he need more attention? She was so busy with her chocolates, maybe he misbehaved to make her notice him.

Questions prickled at the back of her neck as she pondered the possibilities. She looked into Cory's widened eyes. "That sounds acceptable. What kind of work?" She'd already heard Todd's explanation but she wanted Cory's take on it.

Jenni listened to Cory's tale of woe. But in his voice she sensed the same hint of curiosity or anticipation, whatever it was. The penance seemed positive. "I think you can handle that. Don't you?"

He nodded, but his attention shifted to the doorway, and Jenni glanced over her shoulder. Todd leaned against the doorjamb.

"When should we begin?" he asked Jenni. "I know this depends on your schedule."

Since she had to be there, it did, and in part she resented it, which was her own paradoxical reaction. "How about Monday after school?"

He nodded in agreement but didn't make a move to leave.

Jenni pulled her gaze from him to Cory. "How about finishing your homework? I'll have dinner in a half hour or so."

He shrugged. "Can I have some more cookies?"

"How about fruit?"

He screwed up his face with disapproval but headed for the fruit bowl and grabbed an apple, polishing it on his shirtsleeve as he left the room.

Jenni waited a moment until he was out of earshot. "How'd it go?"

"Sullen silence for a while, but I had a few things to say that caught his interest. I think he understands why he's paying me back and what the other ramifications could be."

Another police report, Jenni knew. "Thank you," she said, although her thanks felt somewhat begrudging.

Jenni wanted to get dinner, but Todd didn't seem to be moving toward the door. She tried to think of a nice way to tell him his time was up. "Anything else?"

He pushed himself away from the door frame and jammed his hands into his pockets, but instead of turning away, he stepped deeper into the room. "I'd like to hear more about your business." He crossed to a kitchen chair and rested his hands on the back.

Jenni clamped her jaw to keep it from dropping open. "My business. What about it?"

"Do you mind if I sit?"

She did, but now he'd aroused her curiosity. "Go ahead, but I hope you don't mind if I work on dinner." *And if you do, Mr. Bronski, you can put on your suede jacket and leave.*

"Please do. I don't want to hold you up."

She stuck her nose in the refrigerator, searching for something to prepare but realized she was too unsettled to concentrate. What did he want to know and why? When she spun around, she uttered her thoughts aloud.

Todd grinned. "I suppose I do sound nosy. I might be—I—I know someone who might like to invest in a business. I thought I could give him an idea what you're looking for."

She studied him. He didn't blink an eye, and she calculated he was telling the truth. "You know someone who has money to invest?"

"I do."

Jenni closed the fridge door and crossed to the table, then pulled out a chair and sat beside him. "I began my business full-time about three years ago. With Cory in my life, working outside the home was so difficult. I was already selling the candy to friends and acquaintances on a part-time basis. Word of mouth is a wonder. When my friends and their friends started calling for pounds at a time—for gifts and special occasions like weddings and showers—I couldn't handle it alone. I had to give in and rent space and hire extra help. Finally I turned the basement into my candy kitchen, and during the slower season, I do it all here."

"Renting space must be expensive."

"No. A neighborhood church rents me their

kitchen during the week. No one there uses it, and the cost is very reasonable."

Todd dragged his fingers across his jawline. "So why do you need a partner?"

"Besides the city's pressure, I'm getting more orders than I can handle in this kitchen, and I'd like to hire more help, but I don't want strangers in my home. The church cooperates, but if that falls through and it's a busy season, I'd be in a mess. I've begun to establish a name for myself. I've provided chocolates for numerous parties. I just need financial backing to open a store."

"So that's why you want a partner—just for the money."

"Basically. I figure it's spring, the slow season now that Valentine's Day is over. Then, there's Mother's Day, but after that, the next big selling time is the holiday season. If I lease a building and get settled by August, I'll be ready for the holiday orders to start rolling in."

"I can't believe you make a living wage doing this."

She swept her arm in a broad gesture. "I have a roof over my head and clothes on my body. If you check out the fridge, I have food." She paused and chuckled. "Food that I should be preparing for dinner."

Todd glanced at his watch. "Sorry. I'm keeping you." He pushed back the chair and rose. "Do you have a financial report ready for an investor to study?"

"I do." Her pulse kicked in. She'd stretched the truth a little after hearing his know-it-all questions. She didn't mention she also had savings that she dipped into on numerous occasions between the holiday seasons. But she had ideas and ways to expand, and Mr. Bronski didn't need to know all the details. She would share that with his friend, if it came to that.

She followed him into the living room and waited while he shrugged on his jacket. It did look nice on him. His trim body with broad shoulders seemed to fit the style, and she liked the way he wore his dark hair, short and spiky on top. Neat, but fashionable. If she were looking for a man, he'd be a good prospect. But she wasn't and would never be, not with her health issues. Anyway, she'd gotten used to the idea of being single.

"See you Monday," he said, opening the door.

She nodded. "We'll be there."

"With bells on," she muttered as the door closed.

Todd handed Dale a cola and sank into his favorite chair. "So that's how it went at the Bay Breeze interview." He raised and made a looping gesture. "I'm still up in the air, but it's something, and I want to say thanks for giving Ian Barry the call. We talked about you for a few minutes, which broke the ice."

"You're welcome, but I'm disappointed that it's only a part-time position."

Todd shrugged. "So am I, but he said it could work into full-time once he and Mr. Somerville see how it goes. Obviously if I'm not generating new customers, I'm not earning my keep."

Dale took a lengthy drink of the soda and set his glass on the lamp table. "I suppose you could pick up another client, too, if they have no qualms."

"Possibly, but I'm still giving serious thought to investing in that candy business." He glanced through the large front window. "In fact, she should be here any minute. Her nephew is working off his sentence for stealing my laptop."

Dale drew back in surprise. "You're kidding."

"No. I felt sorry for the kid. And for her, too. She's got her hands full."

"Wish I could stay and see this, but I need to get moving," Dale said, reaching for his glass and downing the rest of the soda. He returned the tumbler to the table and stood.

Todd followed him across the room as the doorbell chimed. "I bet that's them." He quickened his pace, then paused. "Listen, don't mention I'm interested in her business. I haven't told her yet."

"Mum's the word," Dale said, slipping on his windbreaker.

Nodding his thanks, Todd opened the door. Jenni stood on the porch with Cory at her side. For a fleeting moment, the boy looked innocent and scared, but in a flash, his impudence returned. Todd's heart sank.

"Come in," he said, pushing open the door.

"If you have company, we can wait or come back." She gestured to the car in the driveway.

"No, he's just leaving. Come on in."

Jenni's gaze shifted toward Dale who stood in the foyer archway.

"Dale Levin, this is Jenni Anderson and Cory."

"I know you," Dale said, his voice filled with surprise. He extended his hand toward her.

She accepted his handshake but looked at him with a puzzled expression. "You know me?"

"I bought some of your candy at the Streetfest last year and then dropped by your house to pick up a couple of boxes some time after that."

"I'm sorry," she said. "I have so many people in and out buying candy I don't always remember."

"I can understand that." He gave her a grin. "I'll be on my way." He grasped the door before Todd closed it. "Glad to hear about the job, Todd." He gave a wave and stepped outside.

Todd gave the door a final push and turned to Cory. "Are you ready?"

Cory shrugged. "No."

Jenni flinched at the boy's comment. "You'd better be."

"No, that's all right," Todd said. "Not everyone's ready to work. They do it because they have to."

He rested his hand on Cory's shoulder. "And you have to."

Cory's head drooped. "What do I have to do?" Cory mumbled.

"Today you'll help me pick out a dog."

His head flew upward. "A dog? A puppy?"

"Maybe. We'll see what they have at the humane society."

"What's that?" he asked with a concerned look.

"A place where dogs go when they don't have a home."

Cory seemed to ponder Todd's comment. "What happens if no one wants them? What happens if it's a bad dog and chews things?"

"Some people are willing to take the chance and give the dog a lot of love to see if it'll become good."

"No one would love a bad dog," Cory said.

"Someone could, but if not, the dog may not find a home."

"Then would it live at the human soci—"

"*Humane* society."

"Do they live there forever?"

"No. They put the dogs to sleep."

"Kill 'em?" The boys eyes widened the size of golf balls.

"I'm afraid so."

"If I were a dog, I'd want to be good."

"Smart boy," Todd said.

Still standing in the foyer, Jenni listened to the

conversation, irritated that Todd would tell Cory the dogs might be put to sleep, but as she thought about what had just happened, she realized that Todd had demonstrated a lesson to her nephew. Being good has greater rewards than being bad. She hoped the discussion had value.

"Are you ready?" Todd asked Jenni.

"As ready as I'll ever be," she said, wishing she could be home making chocolates.

Todd slipped on a lightweight jacket, and they headed outside. He unlocked the SUV, and they climbed in.

"Hook your seat belt, sport," Todd said, eyeing Cory over the seat back. "I don't want to lose you."

Cory seemed to consider Todd's words as he hooked the seat belt. Jenni attached hers while Todd turned the key in the ignition, and they were on their way.

The humane society was a few miles outside the Loving city limits, and as they drove, the conversation was sparse.

"What kind of dog are you looking for?" Jenni asked when they reached the highway. "Big or little?"

"Big," Cory said from the backseat.

Jenni glanced behind her and saw the child's face look less sullen than it had in days.

Todd gave a one shoulder shrug. "Size isn't the question. Personality is."

"What's that?" Cory asked.

"Behavior," Todd said. "Is the dog friendly? Is it lovable?"

Lovable. Jenni's heart skipped a beat. If Cory could only understand what was being said. People were drawn to animals and people who were lovable.

"We'll know," Todd said finally. "Anyway, you don't really pick the dog."

"You don't?" Cory said.

"I think it's more like the dog picks you."

Jenni smiled, hearing the truth in his words. Cory fell silent, she hoped pondering what had been said. Her own mind shifted back to Dale Levin. If he were a good friend of Todd's, then maybe she didn't have to worry about Cory being alone with him. So far, he seemed an okay guy.

Jenni's thoughts shifted to Dale Levin's comment about Todd's job. Unable to quell her curiosity, she asked, then listened as Todd explained the Bay Breeze part-time job offer.

"I know Philip Somerville and his wife," she said when he finished. "They go to Unity Church. They're a very nice couple."

He gazed at her without saying anything.

"And part-time's better than no time, don't you think? At least until something better comes along."

"It's a beginning, but I can't live on it forever."

"That's obvious." She thought about her own dwindling account.

"I was wondering—" He stopped midsentence.

"Wondering?"

"About taking a look at your financial records. This person I mentioned sounded interested in investing."

The news jerked her to attention. "Really?"

"It all depends on your financial statement, your plans and whether or not you can come to an agreement."

He'd pulled her string again with his know-it-all comment. "I realize that." She gave him a look." So who is this person? Man, I assume? Does he have a name?"

"He does." He gave her a wary look. "Todd Bronski."

She felt her jaw drop, and she didn't try to right it. Todd Bronski. No. No. *No.*

Chapter Five

"Look, Aunt Jenni!"

"Don't be too rough." Jenni shoved her hands into the pockets of her lightweight jacket and watched Cory toss a stick toward Todd's new dog.

He'd selected a cocker spaniel, or as Todd had said earlier, the dog had selected him. It was the same one Cory had latched on to immediately. Jenni had to agree the animal had those sad eyes that looked at her from a roan-colored muzzle bordered by pendulous ears, the kind of look that captured her heart.

"This doesn't seem like punishment to me," Jenni said, witnessing the joy in Cory's face.

"It will be."

His assured comment captured Jenni's curiosity. "Explain."

"That dog needs grooming. It's tedious, and then

there's cleaning up the yard after the dog. Cory will be a super-duper scooper when I get done with him."

Jenni felt her nose wrinkle with her chuckle. "When you put it that way, you're probably right. But only for two weeks."

"I know," Todd said, with his own crinkled expression.

"Cory's wanted a dog for the past couple of years, but I knew he wouldn't feed or care for it when the excitement wore off. Then, you know what?"

Todd rested his hand on her shoulder. "You'd be the dog-keeper."

She felt the warmth of his hand; his gesture felt nice. "You got it."

"But the experience will give him a taste of what he's in for if you allowed him to have a dog."

"Good poin—"

"Mr. Bronski," Cory said, bounding toward him with the cocker spaniel on his heels, "she doesn't have a name."

Todd gave a shrug. "What should we call her?"

Cory crouched beside the dog a minute, then lifted his eyes to Todd's. "Lady, like in the movie."

Jenni smiled. Cory loved that film, and she understood how the name came to mind. "I like it."

"I guess she's got her name," Todd said, ruffling Cory's hair.

"Come here, Lady," Cory called, racing back into the yard. The dog followed as if she knew her name, but Jenni realized the dog had responded to the attention.

"Let's go inside," Todd said, rubbing his arms from the spring chill, then gesturing toward the back door. "You're probably getting cold, and Cory's enjoying himself." He gave Cory another glance. "At least for now."

He had that right. Cory's behavior jumped from good to horrible in a moment's notice. He'd been a tremendous kid until he turned about six—sometime after he'd begun school full-time—from what Jenni could remember. She had never understood what caused the difference.

She followed Todd through the doorway and into his kitchen. Her gaze swept the small area, noticing, for one thing, a large spice rack. Spices meant he cooked or perhaps he had a girlfriend who did. She wandered to the rack, noting the variety—garlic, rosemary, dill, basil, cumin, chili pepper. "It looks like you cook."

When she spun around, he was so close she caught her breath. His brown eyes turned down at the edges and directed her attention to the crinkle lines that formed when he grinned with amusement.

"Sure do," he said, giving her his I-can-do-everything look. "Mexican, Italian—"

"Polish?" she asked.

"Not Polish, but Mom makes some pretty mean pierogies." He flashed her a broader smile.

For some reason, the comment surprised her. He'd actually admitted he couldn't do everything, and hearing him mention his mother gave her an unexpected take on him, too. He sounded proud of his mom's cooking. She liked that in a man and added it as a plus along with his sense of humor.

Todd seemed to realize how close they stood. He stepped back and flagged her toward the doorway. "We can sit in the living room."

Jenni thought better of it. "I'd rather stay here so I can keep an eye on Cory."

"Then have a seat," he said, giving another look through the window.

The man intrigued her. He'd moved from the big city to a small town on the suggestion of a friend. He'd taken Cory into his life to teach him a lesson, yet something deeper lay beneath it, she sensed.

"Were you ever married, Todd?" Jenni asked, startling herself that she'd been so nervy as to ask.

He paused, his hand suspended on the kitchen curtain. "Once," he said finally.

For some reason, he surprised her and she couldn't stop herself from continuing. "Divorced?"

"No. She died in a plane accident. A five-passenger prop."

"Oh, Todd, I'm so sorry."

"It was close to three years ago."

He dropped the curtain and stepped away from

the window, looking as if he wanted her to stop her questions there.

But Jenni couldn't. "What was she like?"

Todd's face darkened and he seemed to withdraw.

"I shouldn't have asked."

His expression looked pinched but he shook his head. "I'm over her death. It took time, but then you know that from your experience." He rubbed his hand across the back of his neck. "Tesha was beautiful. Gorgeous, really. She'd been on her way to a modeling assignment when the accident happened."

Tesha. Gorgeous. Jenni's heart kicked against her chest, overwhelming and disheartening her. A model. Body beautiful. She gazed at Todd, terribly aware of his attractive face and well-built physique. What had she expected from a handsome man, but a gorgeous wife?

Silence settled over them, and absentmindedly she lifted her hand to her chest, realizing how scarred and imperfect she was. She thanked God she wasn't competing against other women in the hope to find a husband.

"I'm sure it's been difficult," she murmured, realizing how much time had passed since either had spoken.

"What about you?" he asked.

His question jolted her. "Single always. Caring for a child isn't conducive to dating." She wouldn't mention her illness, especially now.

"Hard to believe," he said.

"Why? Does a woman with a child interest you?"

He swayed his head from side to side as if thinking. "That depends, I suppose."

Depends on what? Jenni asked herself, but she decided to stop posing questions or he'd begin to probe into places she didn't want to go.

"I wonder how Cory's doing," she said, beginning to stand, but Todd stopped her.

"I'll check." He rose before she could and sped to the window. "He's fine."

He came back toward the table. "And so's Lady." He gave her a smile and sat again, resting his elbow on the table, then propping his cheek against it. "Let's get back to your business."

"What about it?" she asked, amazed that they'd gone full circle before returning to his startling announcement.

"Tell me what I should know. What would you tell any businessman wanting to invest?"

Jenni's heart rose to her throat. "I'm not sure you'd really want to invest in a candy store." Why did she say that? With the business getting more demanding, she needed an investor so badly.

His brows lifted, but otherwise he didn't move. "Why do you say that?"

He ruffled her concentration with his unsettling eyes. If he hung around the candy kitchen, she'd probably scorch every batch of chocolate. And him hanging around was the very thing she worried about. She cleared her throat, hoping to steady her voice. "I'm looking for an investor without strings."

"Strings?" He grinned. "You mean like *apron* strings?"

Jenni controlled her grin. "I suppose you can put it that way. I'm looking for a silent investor, not someone who wants to be in the kitchen." Watching his changing expressions, she could imagine wheels turning in his mind.

"I have no interest in the kitchen, but—" A determined look flew to his face. "I expect to be involved."

Her heart vaulted, seeing something hidden beneath his expression that made her nervous. "And what does 'involved' mean?"

He finally lifted his cheek from his hand and straightened his back. "For example, my expertise is marketing. You'll want help along that line—that is, if I decide to invest."

"Marketing?" Possibly. The hours she spent running around and making presentations to possible retailers marched through her mind.

He rose again and wandered to the window, then turned to face her. "What do you think?"

"When I have a retail shop, marketing wouldn't be quite the same problem. People can purchase the candy there without my beating on doors and hoping a gift shop or a department store will carry it."

"Why not?" He drew back his shoulders and stretched his spine to its full height. "If people buy your chocolates in a department store and like what they buy, next time they'll visit the shop for your candy." He stepped toward her again and settled into the chair. "After you gain a good reputation, you don't have to depend on the other stores."

"I already have a good reputation, Mr. Bronski."

"Todd. And I'm not arguing that point. A reputation can grow, not necessarily get better. Do you understand?"

Jenni did, but wished she could separate being impressed with what he said from being impressed with him. His deep smile lines hid the hint of a dimple, and when he grinned, his eyes sparkled in the most impish way. She wasn't used to a man with quick wit, not one who captured her interest with his gaze.

She rose and pushed her chair in. "I need to give this whole idea some thought. I'd always hoped my partner would be a friend, someone I've already established a relationship with, someone I can trust. Not a perfect stranger."

His face brightened liked the sun. "You have that half-right." He rose and moved to her side.

She squinted at him. "Half-right?"

"Perfect is correct. I am that. But a stranger? No. Your nephew stole my laptop. You know me well."

Jenni struggled to hold her grin at bay.

"And as for friendship," he continued, "only time will tell. You never know what the future may bring."

Jenni brought her pulse under control. She grasped the chair back to steady herself, then stepped toward the window as if checking on Cory. Instead she checked on her good sense. "I wasn't prepared for a business meeting today. I thought we were dealing with Cory's situation."

"Time's fleeting," Todd said. "You never know when the city fathers will put their foot down. Or is it their feet?"

His dimple flickered again, and she wanted to scream.

"I need to give this prayerful thought," Jenni said, "and I realize you want to look at my financial records." She forced a direct gaze. "Just as I need to study yours."

"Definitely," he said with his toying grin.

She continued without comment. "And we need to discuss philosophies, business ethics, goals—"

"Short-range and long-range," he added.

He had the ability to muddle her thoughts with a look, making her realize the truth. "The more I think about this, the more I doubt if it will work."

Todd raised his hand to stop her. "Don't jump to a decision. Let's meet next week. We'll set a time, look at the finances and talk through all those things. If you don't like what I have to offer, I'll gracefully bow out. What do you say?"

She studied his face, wondering if a partnership between them made any sense at all. Sure, he was witty and seemed genuine, plus he'd told her he was an expert in marketing, but was that what she wanted? Jenni turned her eyes from his gaze, facing her real problem. She needed a man in her life like she needed another troubled nephew.

"Let's shake on it," he said.

She felt her eyes narrow.

"Our meeting, I mean. You set the date and time. I'll be there. Account books in hand."

She definitely needed to pray about this, but she could agree to meet at least. He was right about the city's pressure. "Okay, it's a deal," Jenni said, placing her hand in his. Todd's gentle squeeze made goose bumps roll up her arm. She could at least give it some thought while she waited for God's guidance.

When she attempted to withdraw her hand, he held it secure for a moment. "Let's call it a 'sweet' deal."

Jenni got the joke, but she wasn't laughing. She pulled her hand from his and lowered it to her side before she remembered to breathe.

After a lengthy meeting with Todd to look over finances, another letter from the city motivated Jenni to accept his offer as an investor. The city council had only given her until August first to close the business in her home, and time wasn't on her side. She and Todd hadn't fully discussed short- and long-range strategies or goals, but she took the city's letter as a direction from God to accept Todd's offer, and she prayed she hadn't misunderstood the Lord's guidance.

Wisdom poked her with "should haves." She should have done more research, should have gotten to know him better and should have included their goals and plans in their agreement. But she hadn't, and now she'd face the consequences. Today they'd planned to cover some of the issues in another difficult meeting.

Jenni looked into the bathroom mirror to check her lipstick. Looking back at her, she saw a pale face and dazed eyes, as if the whole situation had unsettled her. She pulled out the hairbrush and gave one more swipe, trying to tame her long hair into some kind of knot. The fine strands slid from its clasp and fell in tendrils around her face. Giving up, Jenni tossed the brush into the drawer and slammed it closed.

Standing back, she gazed at her torso. She hated her body and wondered if any man could find her attractive. The question disappointed her. Jenni had thought she'd accepted her tragedy and resolved her feelings. At the time of her surgery, she'd been too depressed by her sister's death and too preoccupied with news that she was to become Cory's guardian to worry about anything else.

Disbelief had flooded her the horrible day she received the call. Kris was dead and she had truly become Cory's guardian. Years earlier, when she'd been excited about Kris's request to be Cory's guardian if something ever happened, Jenni had thought it was only a general question—the kind parents asked. Not one that would come true.

When Kris died, Jenni knew she couldn't replace her in Cory's eyes, and Jenni had never tried. All she could do was cling to the child, wishing she could go back in time to make things right. She adored the boy with all her heart, but raising him proved to be another story. She'd done her best, but now Cory's problems pounded through her mind. Where had she failed?

And Todd. His image slipped back into her thoughts. She realized her desperation had led her to the partnership, but she prayed beneath it all God had been at the bottom of her decision. Perhaps today after they discussed their concerns she would have a better grasp on the situation.

It wasn't that they hadn't tried to talk early. Time hadn't been kind. Every day she'd sat at Todd's house during Cory's penalty—even the word tore at her heart—Jenni had hoped to talk over the business details, but her plan had fallen by the wayside due to interruptions. If it wasn't Cory's or the dog's antics, something else cut into the opportunity. Twice Todd left the two of them there alone when he began his job at Bay Breeze.

Jenni glanced at her watch and realized time was flying. She gave her hair a sweeping glaze of spray and turned off the bathroom light. She bounded down the stairs, grabbed her handbag and hurried to the car. If traffic were bad, she'd be late, and that wasn't an impression she wanted to leave with Todd. Jenni was going for professionalism and respect for each other's time. If nothing more, she wanted Todd to know she was a woman to be reckoned with.

On the highway, traffic slowed to a stop, and Jenni watched professionalism fly out the window.

She was late.

Chapter Six

Todd wiped the perspiration from his forehead. For some stupid reason, Jenni's question about his cooking skills had niggled in his head, and he'd invited her to dinner. Sure, he had spices, but they came with the rack. It had been a wedding gift when he and Tesha had married. The remembrance caught in his chest. Would he ever get over the sorrow he felt thinking of his marriage?

Todd added cream to the sauce and gave it a stir. He eyed the clock. Jenni was late. It could mess up his dinner, but he was pleased to learn she wasn't as perfect as she wanted him to believe.

He checked the recipe again, then poured the pasta into the boiling water and lowered the heat on the burner. He knew that much. Sure, he'd created a few tasty dishes, but nothing to write home about, so tonight he'd been hoping to outdo himself.

Why did he care at this point? The question had risen in his thoughts numerous times. The contract had been signed, and they were partners, for better or worse.

The thought charged through him like a bull. For better or worse hadn't worked in his marriage, so why would it work in a business partnership? He had no guarantee the agreement wasn't a horrible mistake.

Tonight he had too many ideas and decisions to worry about it, and since he'd accepted the part-time marketing position at Bay Breeze, he now had time to spend with the new venture. The thought excited him. He liked new experiences, and this would certainly be one. He was glad Jenni had gotten a sitter. They needed to get down to some serious business.

Though Jenni expected a silent partner, Todd had other plans while he had the spare time. He figured he not only had a right but a responsibility to guide the business in the proper direction. He could only imagine what Jenni's attitude would be.

When the doorbell rang, he jumped at the sound. "You're late," he said, pushing open the door.

"Something smells wonderful." Jenni ignored his comment as she stepped inside. A heady scent washed over Todd as she moved into the living room. She dropped her sweater on a chair, then headed for the kitchen like a bloodhound following a scent.

Though he might have told her she also smelled

wonderful, he bit his tongue. "It's nothing really." The nothing might bear truth if he didn't get to the pesto sauce and give it a stir.

Jenni slid into a kitchen chair and watched as he finished the preparation. His hands felt as unsteady as his cooking talent, and finally he could unwind when the food was on the table.

Jenni tasted the pasta with ground meats in creamy pesto sauce, a special recipe he'd gotten from a great Italian restaurant, and her praise settled his nerves, knowing he'd pulled it off. He wanted her to think he had some talent in the kitchen, and he felt grateful that a quick call to a friend produced the recipe.

The dinner conversation bounced back and forth like a rubber ball, fast but easy, except for Jenni's prodding questions about his past. He changed the subject, wishing he could ask about Cory's mother, but he feared ruining dinner if the topic were too emotional. He'd save it for another time.

After settling in the living room, Todd introduced the first business topic. "I've been thinking about the name of the shop."

"What's wrong with Jenni's Loving Kisses?"

"How about Jenni and Todd's Loving Kisses?" he asked. The inviting image filtered through his mind. He and Jenni?

Her eyebrows shot upward, and he saw her well-shaped lips pull into a tense line. "It sounds like the title of a B movie."

Sadly he agreed. "Okay, try this. Loving Chocolates. It has a double meaning. The city and the product or a verb and—"

"I get it." Her pitch raised a notch. "I didn't know you wanted to change the business's name. I assumed—"

"I'm thinking of marketing. We need a theme. A name that's memorable."

She stabbed a finger in his direction. "If you're talking marketing, my candy is well established in the community. Changing the name would be out and out…stupid."

Todd realized he'd stepped on her toes with the suggestion and flexed his palm to stop the argument. "I'm looking at this long-term, Jenni. You want to expand, don't you? You don't want to limit yourself to candy kisses, and by the way, you should probably call yours something else. That's what the big company calls theirs. We want something original."

"My kisses are different," she said, her gray eyes growing stormier by the minute.

He held back a grin. Getting romantically involved with a business partner was the biggest mistake anyone could make, but the comment about her kisses being different made him curious.

"Why are you staring at me?" she asked, a flush creeping from beneath her collar.

"I'm thinking." He put a clamp on his thoughts and willed away such images. "Why not forget using first names for the store and spice it up with an adjective? Something that describes the candy. Creamy. Luscious. Gooey."

"Wonderful idea," she said. "Gooey Treats. Gooey Sweets. Creamy Goo. That will really knock the customers on their ear."

"You don't have to get sarcastic. I just thought we could think of something unique."

"I like 'kisses.'" Her voice rose another decibel.

He liked them, too, but he quickly dismissed the thought. Seeing the topic was going nowhere, he knew he'd better halt the conversation. "Let's hold that thought. We have other things to worry about now."

"I agree," she said, then spread out her immediate plans—renting a building, moving the kitchen from her basement to the new location, hiring clerks.

"What about promotion, store decor and display, and packaging, product expansion, just to name a few concerns?"

"Let's stick with the products I already have. With running a new shop, I need time to adjust." She sent him a look with such depth of fear it washed over Todd like a tidal wave. "I want this to be a success. We want it to be, don't we?"

"That's the first time you've said *we*."

Her gaze lowered. "I'm sorry. It's been my baby for a long time. It's difficult to let go."

Todd realized that, but she had to learn. "We can

wait on product expansion for now, but it's a bridge we have to cross."

"I'm afraid we'll have lots of bridges to cross," she said.

He thought he saw tears in her eyes.

Jenni could hardly bear another surprise. Sitting beside Todd in the car, she clutched her hands together, wondering where he was taking her. He'd called it a mystery trip. She called it "irritation."

In only one week, her "silent" partner hadn't closed his mouth. Ideas poured from him like Tahquamenon Falls in Michigan's Upper Peninsula. If Jenni had her way, she'd put him in a barrel and send him and his ideas over the edge on a watery journey.

She had never considered Todd would want to change the name of her business or get involved in new products.

She sidled a glance at his eager expression and wished she could be as enthusiastic.

"Here we are," he said, pulling into a parking lot off Washington Street.

Still puzzled, Jenni climbed from the car and followed him to the sidewalk. He paused in front of a greasy spoon diner, then sent her a sweeping gesture. "What do you think?"

She glanced at her watch. Too late for breakfast and too early for lunch. Seeing the stained curtains and yellowed menu in the window, she was happy about that.

When she looked again at his searching expression, the mystery trip's meaning hit her while exasperation knotted her thoughts. "Don't tell me."

He nodded, but his smile faded as he studied her.

She shielded the bright May sunshine from his eyes and peered through the grease-streaked window, then turned and stared at him. "It's occupied, I'm happy to note."

"But not for long. I talked with a real estate agent. This place is going out of business. It's new on the market, and the owner is closing the doors at the end of June. He's desperate to sell the building, and I told him we were extremely limited on funds, but liked the location and—"

Her fists coiled into a knot and her back stiffened. "First, Todd, don't make deals or offers without consulting me—this is a partnership. And second, we aren't extremely limited on funds and I've *never* seen the place." Her cheeks burned with his impudence.

Todd stuck his hands into his pockets and rocked back on his heels, looking dashed by her comments. "Okay, but it's in a prime location and it's available. We could at least take a look."

He had a point. Jenni lifted her eyes heavenward. *Lord, did I hear You correctly?* When she lowered her gaze, she felt Todd's hand on her arm.

"What do you say? Want to go inside?"

She tried to control her spiraling thoughts. Todd's hand felt warm against her cool arm. He'd meant well, she knew. When she gave it some rational thought, what had he done but try to find an appropriate building? The only thing he'd done wrong was failed to realize that Jenni wanted to be in charge, and if she were honest, she liked to be right.

Todd's smile could turn her into chocolate pudding, but for the sake of the business, she decided to listen.

"Okay," she said, "I can't see any harm in looking."

"That's what I thought," he said.

She heard a tone in his voice she didn't like. She was willing to cooperate, but would he?

Todd sat at the kitchen table and eyed Cory's skateboard leaning against the wall on his back landing. A month had passed and he'd reveled in Cory's improved behavior, but today he was worried. He didn't recall the child owning a skateboard, and an uneasy feeling rolled over him.

He headed to the back window to check on Cory. Today he'd had to force the boy to take the scooper and clean the yard. Each visit made Todd more aware; though Cory loved the dog, he didn't enjoy the duties that went with owning a pet. Jenni had been right about that.

When he felt certain Cory was semi-doing his job, Todd crossed to the counter and grasped the kitchen phone. He'd been pleased that Jenni finally trusted him enough to allow Cory to visit without her being there. He had enjoyed her company but understood she had so much work to accomplish, and having Cory busy in a constructive way gave her a reprieve without worrying. Todd punched in Jenni's number and waited.

"Hi," he said, hearing her voice. "Does Cory own a skateboard?"

"No," she said. "He asked for one, but I said we'd have to see his report card first. Why?"

"He has one now."

He heard her intake of breath. "He must have stolen it from someone."

Todd heard the discouragement in her voice. The situation broke his heart. His brother Ryan began the same way, coming home with things he'd "borrowed" and money he'd "earned." "Let me take a better look," he said, setting the phone on the counter and going for the skateboard.

He glanced at the shiny board, then returned to Jenni. "It's new. The price sticker's still on it."

"New?"

Her single word faded to silence.

"I'll talk with him and see what I can find out, okay?"

"Let me know," she said.

He hung up and studied the board, feeling an empty ache. He closed his eyes, wishing he had the kind of faith Jenni did. She prayed even if she didn't get the answer she wanted. But what good was that?

Todd sensed there was a God. He'd attended Sunday school with friends and neighbors, even his parents at times, but he'd seen so much of their behavior going against the Bible that none of it made sense to him. They told lies and stole money from their parents.

He turned the skateboard over in his hand, running his palm across the surface. Power Ride, he read on its surface. Concern rifled through him as he drew in a lengthy breath and turned to the door.

Cory's head jerked back when Todd called, and Lady gave a leap and knocked him off balance. Cory and the dog landed in a heap on the grass.

"Come here for a minute," Todd called.

The boy's laughter greeted him as he ran toward the back door with Lady tangling his feet.

Todd pushed open the door, and Cory walked in followed by the clicking of Lady's nails on the linoleum. The boy's smile faded when he saw the skateboard in Todd's hands, and Todd's heart sank further, validating he'd come face-to-face with a problem.

"Where did you get this?" Todd asked.

The boy shrugged, his eyes downcast.

"You must know where you got it, Cory."

"I bought it." Their eyes met before Cory looked away again.

"Bought it with what?"

"Money."

"Who gave you the money?" Todd wanted to force the boy to look at him, but he stopped himself, realizing intimidation wouldn't help.

"I earned it."

"Earned it how?"

"I helped a neighbor," Cory mumbled. "I cleaned up after his dog and stuff."

Fear coiled through Todd's chest. Had he really purchased it, and if so what had he done to earn the money? So many horrible visions crashed through Todd's mind.

"It's new," Todd said. "Let me see the bill."

Cory dug into his pocket and produced a store receipt.

This time Cory's gaze didn't flinch, and though still puzzled, Todd felt relief that maybe the child was telling the truth and his only guilt was knowing Jenni had said no to his owning a skateboard. If that was so, she could deal with that problem.

"Okay," Todd said, giving the board a pat. "It's a good one for the money." He tilted his head toward the yard. "You can go out and finish your job." At the rate he was going, Todd figured it could take days.

Todd leaned against the doorjamb and watched Cory tossing a ball to Lady. The child glowed with innocence in the June sunshine, yet beneath he hid a depressing darkness that wrenched at Todd's emotions. What could he do? What could anyone do to help the boy?

His hope lifted as he faced his misjudgment. He'd assumed so many things about the skateboard, and perhaps he'd been wrong. Cory proved he'd purchased it, and earning money from the neighbor, though farfetched, might be true. If so, Todd would rejoice.

Often truth seemed out of reach. Todd longed to know more about Jenni. She'd dragged things out of him he'd hoped to forget. At times he witnessed sorrow in her eyes—something deeper than sorrow—regret, helplessness, fear. One day he hoped she'd tell him more about Cory's mother and more about her own life growing up. Jenni needed to be in control. Todd had seen her demonstrate that so often, and he sensed it was all connected to her past.

He pulled himself away from the window and turned to the phone again. He'd promised her he'd call back. All he could do was hope that Cory had told the truth, and Jenni needed news that would make her smile.

Chapter Seven

Jenni pulled off her chocolate-stained gloves and dropped them in the wastebasket, wondering why Todd hadn't called back about the skateboard. She couldn't imagine it would be good news.

She grabbed her notebook and plodded up the basement stairs, dropping the paper on the kitchen counter. The list of things she had to do overwhelmed her, and she could only be happy that candy sales weren't pressing her. She'd finished the last of her orders and now would have time to organize the move. The store needed to be remodeled and decorated, equipment needed to be purchased and the grand opening needed promotion. That she'd leave in Todd's hands.

She hated to complain about Todd. He'd driven her crazy with ideas, but he seemed devoted to the business and to Cory. That part warmed her heart.

She had to keep reminding him he was a *silent* partner. The man didn't know the meaning of the word.

The telephone rang. Jenni grasped the receiver and heard Todd's voice.

"What do you think?" she asked, after hearing a quick version of his conversation with Cory.

"Do you know a neighbor who has a dog?"

Jenni didn't. "Are you sure he said neighbor?"

"He supposedly earned twenty dollars, helping the man clean up after his dog."

Worry filled Jenni's mind. "Hang on a minute," she said, setting the phone down and heading for her purse. She'd never worried about leaving it out in the open, and she prayed she didn't have to.

She flipped open the latch and pulled out her wallet. She thumbed through the bills, calculating what should have been there. Her blood turned icy as she counted again. Unless she was wrong, two twenty-dollar bills were missing.

She carried her wallet back to the telephone and gave Todd the news.

"I'm sorry, Jenni," he said, his voice so filled with sadness it brought tears to her eyes.

"Me, too. I had hoped the dog and—" And what? And Todd being around? What about the love she'd given Cory? Why? The tears slipped from her lashes and rolled down her cheeks. "I don't know what to do."

"Give it time, Jenni. We'll think of something.

The new store plans are distracting you right now. We have so much to do, and Cory needs lots of attention. It's hard to spread yourself so thin."

"I'll bring Cory home later, and you can handle the money situation. Then we need to focus on the shop. We've already signed the purchase agreement so it's too late to back down now."

"I can't, anyway. I have to get the business out of my house." Tension knotted Jenni's shoulders. Too late to back down. *Too late.* Her life seemed too late. She'd missed out on so much in the past years. So often Jenni wished she could change things—her difficult youth, her sister's death and her cancer. But not Cory. She'd always wanted him in her life.

Marriage was for better or worse. She would never experience that, but the relationship with children seemed the same. Jenni would love Cory for better or worse.

Todd closed his eyes a moment, then opened them. He'd never seen Jenni so tense. The house had quieted since Cory had gone to bed an unhappy boy. The skateboard would go back to the store tomorrow, and Jenni had confiscated what was left of her other twenty-dollar bill the boy had taken from her handbag.

The incident weighted Todd with sadness. His brother Ryan's youthful escapades stabbed his memory. His parents had tossed it off as mischievous, but it had become more than that. Todd racked his brain for an answer. What would make a difference for Cory? The kid wasn't his, but he felt compelled to help if Jenni would let him.

"We need to talk business," Jenni said, coming through the doorway with two mugs of something in her hand.

When she set it near him, he smelled the coffee and grasped the mug to take a sip. He needed energy. He'd lost it earlier in the day when he'd first laid eyes on the skateboard. "Thanks," he said, raising the cup toward her, like a toast.

"'Cheers' doesn't fit," she said, her eyes glazed with sadness.

"I know it's been difficult." His pulse gave a kick as he found an opportunity he'd been looking for. "Maybe this will cheer you."

Her expression didn't change much. Beneath her disappointment he spotted a hint of curiosity.

"Philip Somerville gives a big Fourth of July party for his staff. I've been invited along with a guest."

He noticed a faint pink rise from beneath her neckline. "And who's that?"

"You, if you'll go with me. They say it's a wonderful party, and they'll use the penthouse to watch the fireworks."

She shrugged. "Are you sure you want to take me?"

"I wouldn't have asked."

Finally she gave him a faint grin. "It sounds like fun, and I've always wanted to see the inside of their penthouse. People say it has a great view of the lake. I'll get a sitter for Cory."

"Then you'll—"

"I'd love to go as long as—" The eagerness faded from her voice as quickly as her smile.

"No strings attached?"

She nodded, but something in her look made him wonder.

A strange shyness—or perhaps uneasiness—settled over her. Silence passed until Jenni motioned toward the notebook she'd handed him earlier. "What do you think about the plans?"

"You know more than I do about appliances and equipment." He would give her that credit. "I think we could use one long display case and a shorter one that would butt up to a counter. I think shelving could hold a lot of the boxed products."

She gave him a thoughtful look, and he sensed she wanted to disagree.

Todd knew he was right. "It would save us money, and we could add a third case later when the business grows."

Jenni finally acquiesced to his suggestion but stuck firm on some battles. After much discussion, they'd finally agreed on wall color for the shop and the store layout, at least.

"If you'll order the equipment tomorrow, I'll pick

up the paint and supplies so we're ready when we can get into the building." He hesitated a moment before initiating the next touchy topic.

"That's fine," she said. "So that's about it then."

"Not entirely."

Her head snapped upward followed by a frown. "What else?"

"I need to order the store sign." He noticed her grimace, but charged along. "So we need to agree upon the store name."

Air burst from her lungs. "I thought we'd settled on that. Jenni's Loving Kisses is an established name."

"It's limiting, and it'll only take a note mailed to past purchasers to let them know the name's different but the candy is the same fine quality." He felt exasperated. "This is important, Jenni. We really need to settle this."

"Settle it your way," she said.

"No. I'm willing to listen to your ideas, and we can compromise."

"Changing the name isn't a compromise," she muttered, plopping her back against the chair cushion. "I'm too upset to make a decision."

"Jenni." He rose and sat beside her on the sofa. "Let's talk this through. The quicker the sign is up the faster people will look forward to the grand opening."

Her frustration was glaring and her eyes misted

with tears. Todd couldn't believe she would cry over the name of the store. Not knowing what to do, he slipped his arm around her and drew her closer, but she pulled back and, like a punctured dam, tears flooded from her eyes and ran through her fingers.

Todd felt helpless. He wanted to hold her in his arms and press her against his chest, letting her rid herself of the stress she felt, but she'd pulled away and he figured she was angry. "Jenni, it's not that important. I thought that—"

"It's not the store name," she said between sobs. "It's Cory. It's everything that's changing and making life more complicated!"

He didn't know what else to do but massage her back in small circles as she bent low over her hands. Stung that she'd rejected his kindness, he felt at a loss to help her.

Jenni didn't realize how much her situation brought back his own guilt and awful memories. Today he wouldn't push her. She needed to know where his motive was coming from. One day he'd tell her about Ryan and his family, one day when they'd become closer—if that day ever arose.

While his thoughts wandered, Jenni pulled her shoulders back and wiped the tears from her eyes with the back of her hand. "I'm sorry. I'm not usually a baby."

He longed to tell her it was okay to fall apart, but he saw a look in her eyes that warned him to change the subject. His hand had fallen from her back when she straightened, but he gave her shoulder a squeeze as he pulled it away.

"Let's get back to business," she said, looking at him with red-ringed eyes.

He swallowed his empathy and plowed ahead. "What about the sign?"

"We could drop the 'Jenni,' I suppose."

A moment passed before he realized what she meant. "You mean Loving Kisses?"

She nodded. "I realize you don't like the candy being called kisses."

"I just think you're limiting yourself. I know we'll want to expand to other chocolate candy once the business grows. Look, let's call them kisses. That's fine. I just think that—"

"Okay," she said, "Loving Chocolate. We'll go with that. You mentioned it before. I can live with it."

He grasped her shoulders in each hand and searched her eyes. "Are you sure?"

She nodded. "It's a compromise."

The Bay Breeze elevator glided upward, taking Jenni's heart with it. She'd been nervous since accepting Todd's invitation to the Fourth of July party, and today the event had arrived.

Jenni liked Todd—a lot—and fighting it hadn't helped. Since he'd become her partner, she'd had to spend more time with him than she thought was wise, and he lingered in her mind more than she wanted. He'd been wonderful to Cory and she hated to put a damper on Todd and her nephew's relationship. Cory's bad days and impudent attitude had dwindled so that each day his good side seemed to shine brighter.

But Jenni had to protect herself. Todd had been playful with her, almost flirting, and if Todd truly became interested in her and she couldn't dissuade him, she would have to tell him the truth about herself. He would run like a rabbit, and Cory would be lost. So what would she do now that he'd filled her empty life with his annoying playfulness?

Todd rested his hand on her arm as the elevator slid open, and they stepped into a foyer. The penthouse door stood ajar, and inside she heard the sounds of voices and laughter. Her usual confidence had already faded, and an unwanted case of jitters tumbled over her.

As they stepped inside, delicious aromas floated past, assuring Jenni the kitchen was to her right. She glanced down the long hallway and spotted a dining room table covered with platters and bowls emitting the delectable scents.

"Todd," a voice called.

Jenni looked up and saw a man heading their way.

"You must be Jenni," he said.

"Jenni, this is Ian Barry," Todd said, gesturing. "Ian, Jenni."

He smiled and extended his hand. His shake was firm and friendly, and he helped Jenni feel at ease.

"This is a lovely space," Jenni said, admiring the spacious living area with wide windows opening to a balcony across the front where she saw the last remnants of the sun filtering across the sky in orange and purple shades. "I know the Somervilles from church, but I hadn't met them when they lived here.

"After Philip married Jemma and a baby was on the way, they decided to move," Ian said. "Now it's only used for special guests or events like this."

Jenni eyed the balcony and understood why a woman wouldn't want to live here with a toddler.

"I'd like you to meet my wife, Esther," Ian said, beckoning them to follow.

They headed deeper into the room toward a group of people standing near the sliding-glass-door walls. A breeze blew in from Lake Michigan, and Jenni could imagine the fireworks would be spectacular from that vantage point.

"Esther," Ian said.

A lovely woman about Jenni's age turned to face them. Her short, blond hair curved behind her ear, and her face radiated with her greeting. But Jenni noticed something in her eyes—a sadness she seemed to be trying to hide.

Introductions were made, and the conversation moved to Ian and Esther's son, Tyler—a toddler, Jenni guessed—and the men's work at Bay Breeze.

When Ian dragged Todd away, Jenni stood alone with the attractive woman, feeling at a loss for words.

Esther's gaze drifted, and when she refocused Jenni noticed tears in her eyes. Esther brushed them away and managed to smile. "I'm sorry. I heard some sad news about one of our church members as we were leaving the house, and I'm a little emotional."

"I'm sorry," Jenni said.

"Where do you attend church?" Esther asked. "I don't recall seeing you at Fellowship Church."

"I worship at Unity," Jenni said. She wanted to mention Cory and Sunday school, but the topic would be too complicated and lead to questions.

"Then you probably don't know the Hartmann sisters. They're members of Fellowship. They own Loving Arms."

"I've seen the place. On Washington, I think. A bed-and-breakfast," Jenni said, wondering how that topic slipped into the conversation.

"The call today was about Abby Hartmann. She had another stroke, and her sister, Silva—Sissy to us—said this one was worse. I'm afraid Sissy won't be able to care for Abby alone anymore."

"I'm so sorry," Jenni said. "I'll pray for them."

"Pray for who?" Ian's voice sounded behind her as he and Todd returned.

Esther explained, then continued. "The church

has been planning a surprise party for them here at the resort to celebrate the fiftieth anniversary of Loving Arms. Now I don't know what we'll do."

Ian rubbed his hand across her back, sharing her sadness, and Jenni turned away, not wanting to impose on their private moment.

"I think Philip is impressed with you, Todd," Ian said, his arm wrapped around Esther's waist as he changed the subject.

Todd nodded. "He mentioned he planned to talk with you about my position. I hope that's good news."

Ian grasped his shoulder and gave it a friendly shake. "You know it is." He gestured toward the dining room. "Have you eaten? Philip has some great eats in there."

Todd glanced toward the hallway, then back to Jenni. "Would you like to have something?"

She agreed, and they made their way to the table. "What's going on with your boss?" she asked when they were alone.

Todd shrugged. "He seemed pleased with what I've done. I'm not sure, though, what's up. I can't imagine they would consider my working full-time yet."

"Now would be a horrible time," Jenni said, surprised at her admission and her selfish attitude. His smile unsettled her.

"You don't want my silence anymore?"

"Silence, I want. I can use your help, though."

He slipped his arm around her shoulder and nestled her side to his.

She didn't need to pull away this time. His gesture was teasing and not intimate. Intimacy was what she feared.

The table spread was inviting, and Jenni tasted a few items, but soon music filtered down the hallway, so she finished her food and left her empty plate on a serving cart along the wall.

Todd led her back into the great room, and the conversation buzzed. Todd drew her closer and guided her across the floor to introduce her.

Jenni felt the pressure of his hand on her back, a gentle touch that dragged out her concern. Todd wasn't the problem. His dark hair and clean-shaven skin glowed in the soft lighting. His smile was gentle and his eyes glinted with pleasure. She was the problem. She didn't want to feel the emotions she felt at this moment. The closeness was too familiar, and Jenni had nothing to give to a relationship.

She drew away and noticed Todd's puzzled expression. "Let's go out on the balcony," she said.

His hand remained against her back, guiding her forward through the clusters of people. As they stepped onto the balcony, the refreshing, lake-scented breeze ruffled her hair and the skirt of her dress.

Jenni followed the line of the horizon, dark blue

ripples against a deep orange-and-slate background. The sun lowered as she watched—not speaking, only thinking—until it sank beneath the water, leaving a sliver of burnished copper separating the earth from sky. "It's breathtaking," she said, breaking the silence.

"You are," Todd said.

His words caught her off guard, and her legs felt like gelatin. She grasped the railing, afraid to look in his eyes, not knowing if he was teasing or serious.

"You're a beautiful woman, Jenni. You turn heads, and I don't think you even know it."

She looked finally and saw nothing but sincerity in his expression. "I'm not comfortable with compliments about my looks. You can tell me my candy is delicious. I can handle that."

"You should handle a flattering comment about your looks, too. I'm not giving you a line."

"I know that," Jenni whispered, watching the darkness blanket the earth with each tick of the clock.

"I know you said no strings for this evening," Todd said, slipping his index finger beneath her chin and forcing her gaze to his. "I'm not looking for anything tonight, but you're an attractive woman, Jenni. I enjoy looking at you."

She wanted to say she enjoyed looking at him, too, but she could only allow herself to admire him silently. "I worry that—"

"Don't worry, sweet Jenni." His finger left her

chin and brushed along her cheek. "I know we're business partners, and we don't want to do anything to muddle that relationship."

"That's true," Jenni said, hoping he really understood.

"But don't be afraid to give our friendship a try. I won't hurt you…or Cory, if that's what worries you. I feel committed to the boy."

"That's what I want to understand," Jenni said. "Why?"

"I see good in him. Everyone has good in them. Cory just needs to dig down and let it rise above his troubles."

And so did she, Jenni realized. "Thanks for caring about him." She felt uneasy and lowered her eyes as she spoke. "I mean that."

In her peripheral vision she saw him nod. She found the courage to look again, and in the light filtering from the house, she could see an unexpected tenderness on his face. Jenni knew he had more to say, but not tonight, she guessed.

A sizzle echoed over the water, and a powerful blast ricocheted into the sky. Jenni jumped with the sound, and Todd drew her closer, standing behind her as the sky filled with spirals of burning color. She heard the guests moving out to the balcony and gathering along the railing.

In the sky, the bright lights faded to ash and drifted down as another burst rebounded into a chrysanthemum of golden fire sprinkling down over the lake. Todd stood behind her while the sky filled with firelight, splaying and swirling into the dark heavens, taking Jenni's emotions on a spiraling journey of hope and fear.

Chapter Eight

Jenni retreated down the church aisle and stepped outside. She looked into the blue sky, still envisioning the glorious fireworks she'd witnessed at the Somerville party the previous Monday. The evening had been special, yet left her with apprehension. Todd made his intentions clear, yet beneath them, Jenni sensed he hoped for more—but she couldn't reciprocate. Partner and friend was her limit. Girlfriend was not an option.

As Jenni descended the church steps, a pleasant breeze drifted through her hair, and she drew in a lengthy breath. Since July had arrived, the weather had gifted the town with balmy days, and it pleased her. Less humid weather would make working in the new store much easier the following week, but it also meant spending more time with Todd. The thought set her on edge.

She struggled with her feelings as the idea unsettled her. Since the fireworks, she could picture his face in the evening light, feel the touch of his hand against her back and sense his warm breath against her neck. Jenni had been through enough problems for a lifetime. Getting involved with a man had never been a concern before, but she'd never been in the position of spending so much time with one.

Todd had stepped into her life, and he'd awakened feelings she hadn't felt in years. When she'd fallen apart over Cory's stealing from her wallet, Todd had tried to take her in his arms. She'd pulled away, a natural reflex, but what frightened her was that she wanted to be in his arms. Despite his hurt feelings, he'd offered her comfort by caressing her back, and the tender emotion had mingled with her fading tears.

At the party, he'd embraced her again. She'd struggled to keep her distance, not allowing him to hold her close or to rest his cheek against her hair, but she'd longed for the feeling.

Todd was too handsome to settle for a damaged woman. She had nothing to offer him, but how could she tell him so without soliciting his pity? Their business partnership seemed the only way she could deal with his presence in her life, keeping their relationship purely professional.

Jenni's memory slipped back to the lessons she'd heard during church, and the message niggled her thoughts. When the pastor read from Proverbs, she'd felt nailed to the seat. "Charm is deceptive, and beauty is fleeting; but a woman who fears the Lord is to be praised."

Shame covered her when she realized she'd spent too much of her life worried about her figure—or lack of it. She'd missed church too often and had neglected her Bible when her business took all her time. God only became her mainstay in times of trouble. She needed to change that.

No matter how hard she prayed, tension still pushed its way into her days. Cory had accepted his punishment of no skateboard until he earned the money from Jenni. He'd whined and slammed doors, but she'd ignored him, wanting to avoid giving him attention for negative behavior.

Jenni wondered if Todd could be right about that. He'd advised her to give him lots of attention for the good things he did. It seemed like common sense, but sometimes, she had to admit, she was so relieved when he was behaving well she didn't want to stir the pot and bring things to a boil again. She feared if she made a comment he would realize he hadn't been bad for a while and would do something to make up for lost time.

She'd spent the past week deciding a plan for Cory that she hoped would work. She would give him an allowance of five dollars, but for each offense, she would deduct money. If he wanted the skateboard, he would hopefully be well behaved enough to earn it. Today she would explain her plan, and in four weeks, he could own the skateboard.

With Cory on her mind, she rounded the corner of the church building and spotted him standing near the Sunday school entrance. She beckoned, and he hurried toward her.

"What's 'covet' mean?" Cory asked when he approached.

Jenni paused before moving across the church driveway. "It means wanting something so badly you're envious."

"Coveting is a sin."

"Did you learn that in Sunday school?"

He nodded, his expression thoughtful. "Why doesn't Todd go to church?"

His question surprised her. "I don't know. Maybe he goes to Fellowship Church or some other one. You'll have to ask him."

"I don't think he goes." He stuffed his hands into his pockets and kicked at a stone as they walked across the church parking lot. "I don't want to go, either."

Jenni let his comment drop. She had no pat answer, and she wanted to tell Todd what he'd said. Maybe he could appease Cory. Perhaps he did go to church, but she didn't think so, either.

Cory's earlier question about coveting stimulated her own thinking. She figured a restaurant seemed like a neutral location for their discussion. "How about a treat? Let's go get a hamburger for lunch."

Cory's face brightened. "Hamburger Haven."

Jenni smiled. "That's as good a place as any."

The smell of paint drifted into the store's kitchen area, and Jenni peeked through the doorway to view once more the warm beige walls below the chair molding and the coral shade of the upper walls. The dark walnut shelving had been ordered and would be arriving in the next couple of days along with the display cases and counters.

Amazed that her dream was coming true, she closed the door to block the paint odor and continued unpacking the new stainless-steel pots, trays and utensils. Even though she'd sorted and stored the old items from her basement kitchen, she had too much to do before she needed to work on incoming orders. A new fear tore through her: would she be able to keep up with stocking the store *and* meeting individual customer orders?

Though stress stalked her, the past few days had been an adventure. The new location was exciting and she'd found a babysitter to watch Cory. She'd decided once things got settled, she might find a job for him at the store to earn money. He seemed to be better behaved lately, and she prayed it was a new beginning for him, too.

To her relief, Todd was doing what he promised—

marketing. For the past week, he'd finalized a large retail contract, designed and ordered flyers for the grand opening and stayed away from the kitchen. She figured he'd understood her comment about no strings and knew she meant it.

Though she was pleased with his hard work, she feared that if he kept at it she would need to hire more kitchen help. Having someone other than her make the candy didn't sit well with Jenni. She prided herself that the chocolate was homemade, created by her hand alone. Logic said she couldn't keep up with it by herself, and she knew Todd would get more and more involved.

Todd had changed. With their partnership came a new comfort and, even though he irked her at times, she enjoyed his company. What she didn't enjoy were her riled-up emotions. Todd had gotten under her skin as easily as the paint and grime that lodged beneath her fingernails while cleaning and decorating the building.

She pushed him from her mind and concentrated on the work that lay ahead. While the shop had been her focus, the candy supply had dwindled. She eyed her new facility, eager to get her fingers into the chocolate.

Hearing the back door slam, Jenni knew Todd had arrived. She finished loading the last of the utensils into the drawer, and before she could turn, Todd's hand played against the back of her neck.

Surprised, Jenni scrunched her jaw to her shoulder. "Don't pester me like that," she said, swinging around and finding him so close she had to catch her breath. A sweet scent of spearmint filled her senses, and her gaze drifted to his mouth.

"Are you ticklish?" he asked.

She stepped back, but the counter held her imprisoned.

Todd lifted his hand to her heated face. "You are."

"I am not." This time she moved sideways, escaping his grasp. "How did you do today?" Jenni asked, trying to refocus their conversation.

"Very well." He lifted his attaché case from the floor to the counter space and unlatched the lid. "What do you think?"

She took the new flyer from his hand—a brochure, actually—that detailed the August fifth grand opening, listed their chocolate treats and gave a brief history of the business. Pride rose in her, remembering the difficulty she'd gone through to get the business started during a time when she had suffered through so many personal trials.

"It looks good, Todd." When she lifted her gaze from the brochure, her heart gave a flutter. She hated the warm sensation that spread through her when Todd smiled.

"Thanks," he said, taking the leaflet from her hand and slipping it back onto the stack. "I'll need a mailing list of your past customers and I've developed another list of my own. I'll check for duplicates."

"That's great, and I really like what you did with the brochure. I wish I'd done as well. I'm getting more and more behind." She motioned to the counter across the kitchen. "If you have time, I could use help storing the new packaging materials into the cabinets over there."

He glanced in the direction she'd pointed.

"I need to finish putting these pans away and then get busy with some chocolate," she said. "We open in less than a month, and before you know it, we'll have holiday orders."

"It's only July." His chuckle followed.

Todd didn't understand the candy business, but when she lifted her gaze, she caught his playful look.

"I know," he said, "we need to stockpile."

"Don't think I'm not thrilled with all you've done."

He took a step toward her, then halted and a crooked smile flickered on his lips. "And I imagine you'd be even more thrilled if I'd do what you ask."

Without waiting for her comment, he turned to the cartons against the opposite wall and pulled open a cabinet door.

Jenni couldn't help but watch him out of the corner of her eye as he slipped off his sport coat to reveal bare arms beneath his short-sleeved shirt. His muscles flexed as he lifted the cartons, and Jenni paused a moment, admiring his broad shoulders and wondering why she continued to torment herself.

Though she wanted to look away, Jenni couldn't. Lately she'd lain awake at night, thinking about what it would feel like to be wrapped in Todd's arms, to feel his lips against hers, his heart beating against hers, but the image would jerk her back to reality.

She envisioned Tesha's perfect figure in Todd's arms as her imperfect one filled her mind. No man would want her. She knew it, so why did she dream of the impossible? The day the surgeon saved her life, he'd disfigured her—destroyed her body and ended all existence of her feminine self. The loss overwhelmed her.

Todd continued to lift cartons of colorful unassembled boxes and placed them on the shelves. She knew he wouldn't notice her watching him. When Todd focused on a project, he saw nothing else. Jenni wished she could do the same.

Finally she turned back to her own task. When she stored the last large stainless-steel pot, she turned and rested her back against the counter. "Finished," she said, eager to get her mind and energy focused on her chocolate making.

Todd glanced at her over his shoulder, admiring the flush of her cheeks. He paused before turning fully. "How about a break? I can run out and pick up a soft drink."

"I have a fridge full," she said, gesturing toward the new appliance. "I'll take a cola."

Todd set down the carton of salmon-colored packaging and opened the refrigerator, happy to take a break. Jenni was a force to be reckoned with when she wanted a job done. Todd had learned that about her.

When he turned with the soft drinks, Jenni had settled into a chair beside the worktable.

"Here you go," he said, handing her one, then popping the top on his and taking a long, cool drink before pulling out a chair beside her.

"Feels good to sit," Jenni said.

He agreed. "I've been on my feet all day. I had a lot of running around to do for Bay Breeze this afternoon."

She sipped the drink and brushed strands of hair from her cheek.

Though he fought the urge, Todd longed to run his fingers through her silky hair, which shone with gold streaks that shot through the fiery red strands in the sunlight.

He studied her face, realizing Jenni had no idea how lovely she was. So many questions filled his mind, not only about her sister, but about Jenni herself. Why did she look at him with such longing eyes, yet retreat when he touched her?

He had no answer, but he couldn't help but grin, knowing that she thought her sidelong glances had gone unnoticed. But Jenni was wrong. He noticed more about her than she realized, and he planned to keep it that way until he figured her out. *If* he figured her out.

"How's Cory doing with the sitter?" he asked, hoping he might move the conversation to the boy's mother since she wouldn't talk about her own life. With his growing feelings, Todd longed to understand Jenni's background.

"Better than I'd hoped. I thank the good Lord she's a patient woman. She's older and seems to understand Cory's behavior better than I do."

"That's a break." He ran his finger along the condensation that formed on the icy can. "I never asked what he got on his end-of-the-year report card?"

"It came a couple weeks ago. He got a couple of 'less than satisfactory' marks but his teacher moved him into fourth grade anyway. A gift for herself, I think. She didn't want to have him in her class again next year."

Todd chuckled at that.

Jenni shrugged and turned her focus to the tabletop. "She wrote a note. She said he had more good days than bad in the past month." She lifted her gaze to Todd's. "I think I have you to thank for that."

Todd reached across and touched her hand. "No, don't give me all the credit, please. You've worked hard to give him firm love and understanding. Your patience is amazing."

She shook her head, and a tendril of hair fell from its clip and dangled to her shoulder.

The strand mesmerized him, arousing his longing to touch it, to feel it in his fingers and to bury his nose in its sweet fragrance. Todd pulled his gaze away from the wisps of hair when Jenni's voice broke into his thoughts.

"Can I ask you something?"

Her voice sounded so purposeful the question surprised Todd. "Sure."

"Do you ever go to church?"

She'd caught him off guard with that one. "Not lately." The "not lately" phrase meant not in this century, but he hated to tell her the truth. "Why?"

"It's something Cory said after Sunday school last week. He wanted to know why you didn't go to church."

"Lazy, I guess." But he knew it was far more than that. "What did you tell him?"

"I told him to ask you, but what concerns me is he said he didn't want to go, either. I'm afraid he's going to give me trouble now."

Guilt filtered between the cracks in her comments and spread over Todd's spirit. He certainly didn't want to feel responsible for Cory's avoidance of church, but he didn't want to be coerced, either. His thoughts shifted back to Ian. When they'd been alone, he'd asked Todd where he worshiped. Todd had hemmed and hawed, then admitted he didn't attend often. Ian had invited him to Fellowship Church. Was this God doing the coercing?

"He hasn't asked me anything about church," Todd said, pulling his thoughts back to Jenni's concern.

"We'll see," Jenni said, pushing her soda can along the table with her index finger. "I think Sunday school is good for him. I always try to be as good an example as I can, but he admires you so much."

Todd knew he needed to redirect the conversation. "I think you've made great strides with him. He hasn't stolen any money lately or anyone else's laptop that we know." He hoped his comment would be taken with good humor.

"My handbag isn't out in sight anymore," she said. Though she gave him a faint grin, the tension appeared to remain.

Todd brushed his hand along Jenni's arm. "Tell me about her."

A puzzled look flickered across her face before he saw understanding in her eyes. "My sister, Kris?"

He nodded. "I'd understand Cory better if I understood Kris."

She lowered her gaze, and Todd witnessed a horrible sadness wash over Jenni that made his heart ache. "You don't have to," he whispered, not wanting to add any more turmoil to her life than she already had. "Some other time maybe."

To his surprise, she shook her head and looked at him with sad eyes. "Talking about Kris means talking about me. I'm never comfortable with that."

"None of us are, Jenni, and please remember, the past is gone. All we have is today and the future. We do the best we can with both."

Jenni gave him a faint smile, and he shifted his hand to cover hers. The touch surprised him. Her hand felt so small beneath his. Her velvety skin felt cool and soft beneath his palm, and he detected a faint tremble when she looked into his eyes. Then a ragged breath escaped her before she began.

"Kris didn't handle things well after our mother died. We were in our early teens, and we clung together, hurting for our father and feeling cheated. I questioned God's plan, not understanding why the Lord would take away our mother when we both needed her so much."

Todd wanted to speak, to say something to soothe her and let her know he cared. All he could do was press more firmly against her quivering hand to let her know he was there for her.

"Our mother had been the stability in our family, we soon learned. She's the one who took us to church and Sunday school, the one who kept our home in order. Within two months Dad came home with a girlfriend, and within six months he'd married her. She was an abrasive woman who resented Kris and me."

"I'm so sorry," Todd said, letting the words slip from his mouth.

"Somehow I clung to my faith while begging God to explain how this horrible thing could happen. Alcohol became a mainstay at our house—the Christian home where I'd been taught the evils of liquor by my mother."

The details seemed more than Todd could bear. He knew his own youth had been filled with weak Christian morals, demonstrated by his parents. He'd seen his father come staggering home drunk on many a Saturday night, then sit in church with a pious look on his face the next morning. Todd knew the truth. He'd seen more than his share of ambiguous morals to fill a lifetime. He now understood Jenni's attitude toward alcohol.

"Kris didn't handle the situation as well as I did," Jenni continued. "She forgot her faith, or put it on hold, and she went wild. When she learned she was pregnant, she seemed thrilled. She kept telling me that finally she would have someone to love and someone who would love her."

"Did she get married then?" Todd waited for the answer, curious about Cory's father.

"No. I never met the man. When the guy denied his fatherhood, Kris said good riddance. She wanted the baby for her own so she didn't push for support. To be honest, I don't think she knew him that well. It was pitiful to me."

So much seemed clear now as he heard Jenni's story. He could understand her fear of trusting men—fear of trusting *him.* He remembered too well the day he'd pulled her against his chest and she'd resisted. He'd thought it was him, but maybe he had been wrong.

Jenni paused and took a lengthy drink of the soda,

then licked her lips as if they were dry from the emotion of her experience.

"My heart headed in two directions when all this happened. It broke for Kris, who'd backed away from her faith and now had the responsibility of a child without a father to help. I suppose that was of her own choosing. She could have gone to court and insisted on DNA tests, but Kris was just as happy forgetting the man. Despite it all, I was excited about becoming an aunt. I'd have the pleasure of a small child in my life without all the work. I suppose I needed love, too."

Todd heard his own ragged sigh. He lifted his hand from Jenni's and touched her shoulder. "I'd give you a hug if you'd let me."

She shook her head. "I'm all right."

But she wasn't, and it saddened him to see her fight the truth.

"Anyway," she said, easing back into the chair as if she'd caught her breath and rejuvenated her spirit, "Kris wasn't the best mother. She tried, but we'd had no role model after Mom died. Kris liked to party, and so I volunteered to care for Cory. I took care of him so much, he almost seemed like my child."

Tears glistened in the corners of her eyes as she continued. "When Kris died in the skiing accident, I became Cory's official guardian. I'd been recuperating from an illness so I was home…."

Her voice faded and she gave him a hesitant look, fright flickering across her face and then vanishing.

Todd longed to pursue the topic. He yearned to know more about Jenni. What made her tick? What brought fear to her eyes? What was it she had been protecting herself from?

She was unlike Tesha in so many ways. Though Jenni was beautiful in her own way, she never flaunted it. Looks seemed unimportant to her. Instead, she valued kindness and humor. She prided herself for her control and organization, and chided herself for not meeting Cory's every need. How could she? Everyone had weaknesses and imperfections. Everyone made mistakes.

But not Tesha. She had been filled with self-purpose. The world revolved around her own interests. Everyone else was wrong. Jenni revolved around the world and made others her purpose. The two were incomparable.

"That's about it," she said, her matter-of-fact tone not covering the emotion Todd sensed. "After I went back to work, Cory had to go to day care, and then I got the idea to take my part-time candy making and turn it into a stay-at-home career."

Todd realized he'd been sitting ramrod straight, riveted to her plight, and yet still not knowing the event that caused her look of panic. "That explains a lot about Cory. Even young children feel abandoned. First he lost his mother, then you had to return to work. And each time your life gets busier, Cory has an unconscious fear of losing you."

"You didn't tell me you studied psychology." She appeared to relax.

"Every salesman knows a little psychology."

Jenni laughed aloud. "You mean you're using psychology to sell my chocolates?"

"Never. Your candy is so good it sells itself."

Her face brightened, and he felt better. He took a swig of the soda, then leaned down and kissed her cheek.

Jenni's eyes sparked with apprehension before fading to acceptance. "Thank you. I'm glad people love my candy."

"Me, too," he said, knowing it wasn't her candy kisses he wanted, but her kisses. Would he ever experience her soft mouth on his? The question left him wondering.

Chapter Nine

When the back door opened, Jenni turned toward the glaring sunshine and the swish of heat coming into the room.

"Candy," Todd said. "Smells delicious." He trotted across the room and hovered over her shoulder, eyeing the melting chocolate. "How's it going?"

His breath whispered across her neck, and she pushed the straggles of hair away from her face to distract herself. "Okay," she said, hating to tell him Cory's latest caper.

His nearness distracted her, and she sent him one of her knitted-brow looks.

"From that expression, I'd better get out of your way." He backed off and then stopped. "I might just do that permanently, you know."

She turned at his startling comment. "What do you mean?" Her pulse zipped through her.

"I forgot to tell you Ian had the talk with Mr. Somerville. He said they might be ready to take me on full-time at Bay Breeze already. I'll be out of your hair completely. That should make you happy."

When Jenni gazed into his eyes, she realized that wasn't the case at all. "Not when I need your help," she said, to cover her emotion.

She felt his hand press against her back for a moment, then felt her apron unfurl from her body. "Why did you do that?" She grabbed the ties and knotted the strings behind her.

"I'm helping."

"If you really want to help, I'll give you another job." She worked with speed, pouring five pounds of quality chocolate wafers into the large double-boiler kettle. "To be honest, I'm a little upset."

"Cory?"

She nodded. The words hung in her throat. "He punched a kid at the sitter's and took his cupcake."

Todd's expression altered as the words left her mouth. "He's been so good lately."

"I know. The calm before the storm, I'm afraid."

She noticed Todd's face morphing from concern to a halfhearted grin. "The only positive part of it is a cupcake is a long way from a laptop, Jenni."

The fact might have been funny, but it hurt her too badly to admit it. "It's still a slip backward."

Watching his expression, she saw a new worry. "Is the sitter going to let him stay?"

"She didn't say she wouldn't, and I didn't ask. She punished him. He didn't get the boy's or his own dessert, but—"

"Look, it's the same thing again. School's out. You're tied up with getting ready for the opening. You're tired at night. Cory feels left out. He's slid into his old habit."

Todd had made a good point. "I want to bring him here so he can help me, but I want to have enough quality time with him once he comes. I'm sure he can put the boxes together and things like that."

"He would enjoy that. Tell him that if he's good you want him to come and help. That might be all he needs to hear, and I'll try to think of something I can do for him once he's back on the right track. Acknowledge the good and ignore the bad."

Todd shifted closer and put one hand on each of her shoulders, giving them a squeeze. His gaze sought hers, and Jenni felt her knees weaken from his innocent touch. Foolish, she thought, struggling to control the sensation.

"I would really appreciate some help right now," she said, hoping to motivate him to move.

He sidled away from her and leaned against the counter. "I thought I'm your silent partner."

"Since when?" His smile toyed with her thoughts and she needed to concentrate on her work. "Follow me." She beckoned him to a kettle of melting chocolate. "I've been thinking about a new candy, something different from the kisses."

"Aha, you liked my idea."

"What idea?" She realized he'd suggested a new product, but she wasn't going to give him credit for this brainstorm.

"You remember," he said, chucking her under the chin. "So tell me, what creative venture do you have for me?"

"It's batches of chocolate laced with raisins and macadamia nuts, plus my secret ingredient."

His eyes widened. "You never did tell me about that secret ingredient. You said you'd reveal it to your partner. That's me."

She gave him a playful nudge. "A dash of cardamom goes into the chocolate." She lifted a spice jar and sprinkled the brownish powder into the pot. "Get the idea? For Christmas, I'm thinking we could use white chocolate with dried cranberries and peanuts or almonds."

Jenni pulled down a nest of large trays and stacked them on the counter. "Here are the trays and the recipe." She slid the card in front of him. "You understand?"

"Sure thing, boss," he said with a salute.

She lifted an eyebrow for emphasis. "Once you add the nuts and raisins, you'll pour it on the trays. That's it, and it will be really helpful."

He nodded, for once without comment...and minus the salute. She hid her grin and returned to her melting chocolate. As she concentrated on her own work, she envisioned the new candy and wondered if it would be a good seller.

"Does this candy have a name?" he asked from directly behind her.

Jenni felt her apron strings drop to her side again, and she spun around. "Enough is enough." But before she could re-fasten them, he spun her around and grasped the ties. As he worked behind her, she felt his breath graze her neck again, and gooseflesh rose on her arms. She refused to react, sensing it would only encourage further antics. "I'm sure the chocolate's ready by now. Don't let it burn."

He moved back to his task, and let his question drop. She'd been thinking about a name—something that showed a merger of two tempting ingredients, like Friends Forever or Double Trouble—something cute and memorable.

As she concentrated on her confection and worked with the large candy kiss molds, she pushed Todd from her mind. She knew he was following directions when she heard the freezer door open and close as he cooled the chocolates. Jenni relaxed in the silent room.

"What do you think?" Todd asked.

She turned as Todd stepped to her side, jutting a large tray toward her. She gazed down, expecting to see the uniform clusters of raisin-nut chocolate. Instead, her heart slipped to her toes.

"What did you do?" She gaped at the chocolate mottled with raisins and nuts spread out in one large sheet on the tray. "You didn't do clusters!"

"Clusters? You didn't mention clusters."

"But I told you to follow directions."

"I thought you wanted me to spread it on the trays. Oh, well, we can call it Chocolate Surprise and sell it as a new sheet candy."

"Bark," she said.

He eyed her strangely, then grinned. "Woof! Woof!"

Todd knew how to make her grin, and he did. "It's called bark." She released a blast of air from her lungs. "Break your Chocolate Surprise into bite-sized chunks and put it in the storage containers."

He looked disappointed. "Okay, and then I'll get out of here." He took a step backward and then stopped.

"Todd, I'm sorry. Maybe this was God's way of convincing me to introduce another new candy. I'm stubborn sometimes."

"Oh, really?" he said.

She caught the playful sarcasm in his voice. "You never know what God can do to make us change," she said.

He paused a moment as if a flashbulb had blinded him. "Funny, you say that. I've been thinking about church."

"You have?"

"It wouldn't hurt me to go if it'll help Cory. I don't want to feel to blame for—"

"I wasn't blaming you, Todd. I only know he admires you, and that's why I asked you about your church attendance."

"Don't worry about it," he said. "It's a long story. I create my own guilt."

Jenni's curiosity piqued, and she longed to ask what remarkable long story had passed through his mind.

"It wasn't just your question, either. Ian invited me to his church, and I thought I might go."

"They're not members of Unity like the Somervilles."

"No, Ian attends Fellowship."

Disappointment washed over her. "I can tell Cory that you're going there."

"You could come with me. Just for a Sunday. Ian's become a good friend, and Dale goes there, too. I thought I'd be more comfortable—"

"I'd love to come with you." By the look on his face, she knew she'd surprised him. "Cory will, too."

"I'd like you to get to know Dale better, anyway."

"Why?" she said.

"Because we're invited to his and Bev's wedding."

"We?"

"Me and a guest." His dimple winked at her. "I

figured you wouldn't want to miss another good party."

"Okay. I'll go if you do something for me."

"What?" He gave her a suspicious look.

"I'd like to hear the long story you just mentioned. I think it's worth the time, and remember, you listened to mine about Kris."

His mouth opened and closed again as if he planned to protest, but something made him change his mind. "I had a brother just like Cory, and I've never forgiven myself that I didn't do something before it was too late."

Jenni's heart ached hearing the story of Todd's younger brother. Ryan had gone from misbehavior to misdemeanors to drugs to burglary, and Todd felt responsible.

"You said it to me, Todd. We can't be perfect. We do our best. You had no idea that—"

"I had no proof, but I had an idea that Ryan was getting deeply into trouble. I knew he was using drugs. I'd drifted from church, and though I didn't get into trouble, I could have." He grasped Jenni's arms, his look desperate. "I blinded myself to it all, Jenni. I didn't lift a hand to help Ryan. I just focused on my own life."

"I understand," she said, "and God forgives you, Todd. You're making up for it now with Cory. Stop torturing yourself. I see the sadness in your eyes, and it makes me sad."

His hands slipped from their grasp and his arms

dropped to his sides, pinning her with his gaze. "We all have our secret demons, Jenni."

His look slithered through her, and she knew her attempt to hide her fears had failed.

Todd sat outside Ian's office, waiting for their meeting. His thoughts shuffled from the possible job offer to Jenni's past to Cory's question whether or not he went to church.

Cory needed a good, solid role model. The boy had never known a father or grandfather, for that matter. From what he could put together, Jenni didn't date much and had no relatives she talked about, so the boy had only been around women.

For the past week, Todd couldn't shake the image Jenni had painted of her earlier years. He'd thought *his* life had been bad. Jenni's hardships could be multiplied by a thousand. He'd finally told her about Ryan, but she hadn't budged about telling him her secret, and he knew she had one. If he were forthright, he'd have avoided telling her his whole story, too. They both had experiences they had been unable to share. Until they trusted each other, he had no hope of their friendship going anywhere.

He'd joked and teased, like he always did, but beneath his smile, he had ached for Jenni, and he longed to know what else lay hidden in her past. He'd seen the sadness in her eyes again that day—something personal and deep.

For the first time in years, Todd began to think seriously about his faith. He'd gone to Sunday school as a boy, and he'd believed in God. He knew Jesus was God's Son, Savior of the world, but Todd had let that knowledge slide. Instead, he'd gotten wrapped up in worldly things, things that gave him no peace of mind. And when his marriage was so shaky, he realized he'd still clung to the belief that marriage was a promise he'd made to God. He doubted if that thought had crossed Tesha's mind, but then, she didn't worry about the marriage. She worried more about her makeup.

Todd's parents hadn't been that bad. They'd just enjoyed life too much, partying with friends and breaking one commandment after the other—never anything evil, just a disregard for God's Word. So how was he supposed to learn right from wrong? Maybe that was an easy excuse.

Jenni had rarely mentioned her father, and now Todd had begun to wonder if the man were living. Maybe he'd been abusive. Perhaps Cory had seen his grandfather's drunken ranting and those were the child's only memories of an adult male. Even a three- and four-year-old could be affected by unconscious remembrances. But Todd knew he was only speculating. He'd learned very little from Jenni, but what he'd heard had been enough to cause him, even more deeply, fear for Cory's well-being.

If attending church could turn Cory's direction,

then Todd had decided he could go to church. Jenni's faith gave him hope that some people who professed faith actually followed God's Word to the best of their abilities.

He'd noticed the disappointment in Jenni's eyes when he told her he'd go to Fellowship Church. That surprised him, and it probably shouldn't have. Telling Cory he attended and letting the boy see him in church were two different things. Todd felt uncomfortable going to worship with Jenni in a church he didn't know, and she hadn't invited him. Attending Ian and Dale's church made more sense.

Todd eyed his watch, his mind scuffling with questions and doubts. Though he'd looked forward to the promotion to full-time, now the timing seemed so wrong. He almost wished Ian would give him bad news.

His thoughts faded when Ian's door opened and Ian stepped into the outer office with a smile and his arm extended. "Come in. Sorry I had to keep you waiting."

"No problem," Todd said, crossing to him and shaking his hand.

Ian gestured for him to enter the office, and Todd stepped inside while Ian followed.

"Did you enjoy the party?" Ian asked as he sat behind his desk.

"It was great. Good food, great company and unbelievable fireworks."

"I noticed the good company."

"Jenni? She's my business partner."

Ian grinned. "Call it whatever makes you happy."

Todd felt an unexpected flush sizzle beneath his collar. "We're not really dating. To be honest, I wouldn't mind, but she's a don't-mix-business-with-pleasure kind of person. A little standoffish."

"I didn't see that at the party. You two looked pretty cozy on the balcony."

Todd thought back to that night. He'd stood behind her, his hands caressing her arms. He'd loved the feeling, and for once she hadn't resisted.

"Anyway," Ian said, breaking into Todd's thoughts, "I'm glad you had a chance to talk privately with Philip. He's very impressed with your work."

Todd swallowed, letting the compliment settle in his mind. "That's good news."

"I have better news," he said. "Philip's decided to give you a chance at full-time."

The truth had caught up with Todd, and his heart sank. Not long ago he would have celebrated the opportunity. Today he struggled to find the right words to express his feelings.

Ian drew back as a frown settled on his face. "You're not happy?"

"Yes...and no." How could he explain what had been happening in his life? "I'm worried it's too fast. I've done well working part-time, but I don't want Mr. Somerville to be disappointed if I can't keep up the same pace full-time. There's a difference. My current success could be a flash in the pan."

"Right. I thought of that, too, but I figured you'd get discouraged with the part-time, and we'd lose you. I mentioned that to Philip, and he agreed. You're too good to lose."

"Thanks. I'm glad to know he's pleased with my work, but—" Todd drew in a lengthy breath and decided to be more honest. "You know I've invested in the candy store, and we have a grand opening coming up in the beginning of August. I've been doing promotion for the store, and we have so many open-ended plans that need—"

Ian chuckled. "In other words, you might like a full-time position at a later date, but not now."

"Exactly," Todd said. "But I don't want to lose the opportunity, Ian. I have no idea if the shop will go bust or be a raving success. I can only be hopeful, and I know the product is good."

"I'll let Philip know you'd rather have more time to develop the work part-time. I hope I haven't done such a good job of convincing him that he'll disagree."

"Let me know if that happens. The job at Bay Breeze is bread on the table. The candy shop is dessert. You know too much dessert isn't always healthy."

Ian came around the edge of the desk and extended his hand. "Listen, we have a large group coming later in the summer that's from your efforts, and a fishing group already reserved for an autumn outing. That's rooms and boat rentals plus meals. That's good work."

"Thanks," Todd said, shaking his hand and wondering how he had the nerve to turn down a full-time job. He had to be stupid—or in love.

Jenni put the last plate in the dishwasher, closed the door and pushed the button, then arched her back and stretched. She felt miserable. Between the work at the store and her household responsibilities, she felt totally inadequate. Cory's progress had faded, and she noticed again his sullen demeanor and occasional impudent remark. Todd had to be right. Cory feared being abandoned.

Her plan to bring him to the shop had fallen from her memory. She'd mentioned it, then hadn't followed through. Tonight Cory had reminded her, and she felt like a heel. She had nothing to say but sorry. That hadn't been what Cory wanted or needed to hear.

She turned off the kitchen light and stopped at the bottom of the staircase, longing to go up and do something to make things right, but she felt at a loss. Tonight she was the rope in a tug-of-war, jerking this way and that while having no idea which side would win.

Jenni plodded into the living room, kicked off her shoes and snapped on the television. She had no idea what shows were on each Wednesday night. The TV usually remained silent except for Cory's viewing.

Using the remote, she flipped through the stations, finding nothing that caught her interest and feeling lonely. Todd had spent the full day at Bay Breeze. She knew he'd had an appointment that morning with Ian, and that made her curious. Todd mentioned having a later appointment, then tonight a chamber of commerce do while she'd stayed at the store to package chocolate and set up displays.

Time seemed to be fleeting; in a little more than two weeks the store would open. After that she hoped life would calm, at least a little. Jenni actually missed working from her home. Life seemed easier then. Between batches of chocolates, she could do the laundry or run out to pick up Cory from school. Now that she had a store, she couldn't hang a Gone Fishin' kind of sign on the knob every time she wanted to leave.

Car lights flashed across her picture window, and she heard a door slam. Curious, she rose and headed for the foyer, hoping it was Todd. She peeked through the security view, and her heart lifted.

"Hi," Todd said when she opened the door. "You look tired."

She released a sigh, wanting to tell him she was

tired and lonely. She stepped back to let him inside, then closed the door. When she turned, Todd lifted his hand and caressed her cheek. His touch sent a calm rolling down her chest and into her heart.

"Sit," he said. "You rest, and I'll make us some tea."

The suggestion surprised her, and though she rarely drank hot tea in the summer, the idea sounded soothing. She heard him running water and clanking the kettle in the kitchen, then smelled a strange odor like smoke.

"What are you doing?" she called to him, and headed for the kitchen, certain that she'd cleaned off the burners.

"I'm making tea," he said as she came through the doorway, but something stopped her. "Do you smell something burning?"

He closed the distance between them, sniffing the air. Todd's look of concern said it all. Before she could verbalize her panic, Cory's scream pierced her heart.

Chapter Ten

Todd shot past Jenni and bounded up the stairs, blood pumping through his veins and pounding in his temple. Smoke rolled from Cory's doorway, and Todd grasped the door frame and swung inside.

"A fire extinguisher," Todd yelled into the hallway, hoping she had one.

Cory stood beside his bed, tears flowing from his eyes while a fiery blanket flared on his mattress and sent black smoke curling into the air.

Todd grasped a discarded quilt and tossed it over the flames, hoping to smother the blaze that licked its way toward the walls. His attempt seemed futile as the flames surged through the cloth.

Jenni's cries reached him, and her footsteps pounded through the doorway as she flailed the extinguisher toward him, then fell on her knees beside Cory. Her sobs joined the boy's as Todd released the lever and engaged the flame-retardant spray.

Charred cloth sizzled beneath the foam, and the flames struggled for life, then died in a soggy, blackened heap. Todd stared at the smoldering mess as tears formed in his eyes.

He crouched beside Jenni and Cory, drawing them into his arms. Fury ranged inside him, but he smothered it as he had the fire. Anger would do no good now. Only patience and understanding would help the child see what he had done.

Jenni finally drew back, her face smudged with mascara, her eyes rimmed with tears and anguish. She clutched Cory's shoulders. "What did you do?"

Instead of insolence, Cory's face registered his fear and guilt. He opened his hand and a matchbook dropped to the ground. Beside it lay a broken cigarette Todd hadn't noticed earlier.

"Where did you get this?" Todd asked, picking up the tobacco and matches.

Cory sniffled, his eyes downcast. "From a boy."

Jenni lifted his chin and gave him a direct look. "At the sitter's?"

He shook his head. "At the playground. She took us to the park."

Jenni's shoulders sagged, and she turned to Todd, her expression so helpless it wrenched his heart.

"Do you realize what you did?" Todd asked, wanting to shake sense into the child. "You could have burned down the house. You could have been injured, or hurt one of us."

"Cory, I love you," Jenni said, her voice trembling. "I couldn't bear to lose you."

The child's eyes filled with wonder. "I'm sorry," he said.

Jenni cuddled him again. "And look at your room, Cory. It's ruined."

The child burst into tears, and Todd knelt again and drew the two into his arms. He'd never experienced fatherhood, but today he felt like a dad, wanting to give Cory his wisdom, wanting to forgive him, yet knowing the boy had to learn right from wrong. But the lesson wasn't Todd's responsibility. It was Jenni's.

Jenni rose and touched Cory's shoulder, her body still quaking. "Go and wash up for bed, Cory. You can use the guest room. I'll talk to you about all this in the morning."

Todd released the child and rose, watching him tug his pajamas from a wad of discarded clothing on the floor near his closet and plod from the room, his head lowered as if he understood what he'd done.

As he vanished, Jenni fell into Todd's arms, the first time she'd let him cuddle her to his chest. The sadness of the situation dulled the warmth he felt, but she'd yielded to his embrace, and he reveled in her closeness.

"What am I going to do?" Jenni whispered into his neck, seeming unaware of their embrace.

What are we *going to do?* he asked himself, brushing his chin against the silkiness of her hair. "Let's talk downstairs," he said, easing away, lest she realized how closely they stood.

But he couldn't let go. He took her hand and led her from the shambles into the hallway. She stopped a moment to check on Cory. The child had done as she asked and had crawled into bed, probably exhausted from the scare.

They plodded down the stairs, side by side, the news he'd stopped by to tell her seemingly unimportant after the fiery experience.

The teakettle was whistling as they reached the bottom, and Todd hurried into the kitchen, motioning to Jenni to go ahead into the living room. He made swift work of the tea and carried the mugs in to her.

She'd curled up on the sofa, her arms cuddling a throw pillow, with her legs pulled up against her. Todd felt overwhelmed by the look of helplessness that had invaded the moment. He set her cup on the table, then sat nearby in a chair.

The tea was too hot to drink, so he placed it on a coaster and rested his head against the chair back, letting the fright that had assailed him, drift away in the silence.

Jenni finally shifted, curling her legs beneath her before she grasped the mug. She blew on the surface, then took a guarded sip. Her eyes looked glazed, and Todd could only imagine the thoughts that filled her head.

"You'll have to call your insurance company tomorrow," he said, wishing he could say something more comforting.

She nodded as her gaze drifted toward the darkened scene outside the window.

"I wish I could say something wise and helpful, Jenni. All I can offer is a shoulder to cry on and all the support I can give you—you and Cory," he added, because it was the child that needed so much.

Memories took him back to his childhood. He'd probably done things as foolish, but at the moment, none came to mind. His brother, Ryan, had topped his antics a thousandfold.

"Thanks for being here and keeping a level head," Jenni said. "I fell apart. I'm ashamed of myself. I can only thank God that I remembered where I kept the fire extinguisher."

"I'm thankful you owned one," Todd said, trying to send her a comforting smile. It worked, and she grinned back.

"That was a blessing." She drew in a lengthy breath and the release quivered through her body. "I have to find some form of punishment, but something that's meaningful. Yelling and lecturing don't help. They only alienate him more."

"I agree. He's doing better, and you don't want to lose what progress has been made." His mind spun with possibilities, but nothing seemed to strike the right chord, then a new thought came. "I wonder if you could ask a fireman to talk with Cory. I'm sure he'd have stories to tell him, something that would shake his senses."

Her eyes shone brighter when she looked at him. "That's a thought. I'll call the station tomorrow."

"I'm glad about going to church on Sunday. Cory needs to see what it is to be a man, and though I'm not the best example, I'll try to do better."

"You've been wonderful," Jenni said. "What would I have done lately without you? I'd be lost."

She'd brought him back to his original reason for visiting, and Todd used the moment. "By the way, I turned down the full-time position today."

Jenni's back straightened like a ramrod. "You did what?"

"I turned it down. I delayed it, really."

"But—"

"I need to be with you right now…with the business. We'll be open in a couple more weeks. Then things should smooth out, I hope. The pressure should be less then."

"I can't believe you did that for me, Todd."

Todd couldn't believe it, either, but he had. Holding Cory and Jenni in his arms had awakened new feelings in him. He'd been floored by the sensation, realizing he'd become more than a friend. He'd become their protector.

* * *

"What did you learn at the fire station the other day, Cory?" Todd asked as they headed toward the church Sunday morning.

"I saw the fire truck and where the firemen live."

"Was that all?"

Todd didn't hear a sound from Cory, but in his rearview mirror, he could see the boy shaking his head.

"He cried," Jenni whispered.

Todd's heart gave a little tug. "Why?"

"Tell Todd about the things the fireman told you."

Todd listened as Cory related tragedies of families dying, homes destroyed, dogs and cats burned in house fires. "I thought about Lady," Cory said.

"Sounds like you learned a few things," Todd said again.

"Don't play with matches." Cory's voice quaked from the backseat.

Todd glanced into the rearview mirror, worried the child might start crying again. "Good for you. That's the best thing you could learn."

"I was proud of him," Jenni said. "He asked good questions and listened to the answers."

Cory leaned forward, but restricted by the seat belt he could only rest his hand on the back of Todd's seat. "The fireman told me not to take things from strangers because they could be dangerous."

"Like the cigarette?" Todd had worried if the tobacco had been laced with illegal drugs. It wouldn't be the first time.

"Uh-huh," Cory said. "It could be drugs, and I would die."

"That's right," Jenni said. "Never take money or gifts, take nothing from a stranger. I don't think you will do that again." She adjusted her seat belt so she could turn and look at Cory. "I'm proud of you."

"Me, too, pal," Todd said. "The situation was terrible, but it was a good lesson for all of us."

They grew quiet, each in their own thoughts. He hadn't slept well since midweek when Cory had started the fire—a terribly dangerous accident that could have been a tragedy. But he believed Cory had really learned his lesson this time.

And Todd had learned one, too. When he'd gotten home that night, he had searched for his Bible and found it buried in a stack of old books. God had been merciful to them with the fire, and Todd had caught himself praying and thanking the Lord for Cory's safety. Maybe meeting Jenni and Cory had been the catalyst he needed to regain his faith.

Todd saw the church steeple rising ahead of them. "Looks like we're here," he said, rolling into the church parking lot. "I'll let you out by the door, and I'll park."

He found a spot and hurried across the pavement. Inside, the vestibule seemed dark to Todd because he'd just been in the bright sunlight. But when he focused, he saw Jenni and Cory talking to Esther and another woman holding a baby.

Jenni spotted him and gave a wave. "Todd, this is Annie DeWitt and her new son, Dillon. You already know Esther."

"Hi," Todd said, offering both women a handshake.

Cory stood beside Jenni, and Todd could see the boy was watching his every move.

"Esther just mentioned that Philip would like to talk with you about a candy order."

"Really?" He wondered if her comment had a punch line, but Esther answered his question.

"It's a party for the Hartmann sisters—kind of a mixed bag. Jenni will explain."

She'd left Todd in the dark with her explanation, but he smiled and agreed to hear the story from Jenni.

"Time we find a seat, I suppose."

Cory slipped his hand into Todd's, making Todd's pulse lurch. Jenni joined them, and they headed down the aisle. Todd felt as if they were a family, but he feared if Jenni had anything to say about it, they would never have a chance to be one. No strings. How many times had she stressed that?

They slipped into a middle pew and sat with Cory between them. He hadn't let go of Todd's hand, and finally Todd gave it a squeeze before releasing his grip to pick up the hymnal. Cory copied his every move.

Todd let his gaze drift in front of him, then gave a subtle look over his shoulder and caught Dale's eye. His friend gave a nod, and he winked back, again amazed that he'd agreed to attend worship. As his gaze settled on Cory, he knew the boy had been one reason he'd come, but in his gut, he sensed he'd been guided there for his own need, as well. Jenni always said the Lord had a plan. Todd sensed this was part of it.

The service began as Todd remembered—hymns, prayers and Bible readings. One reading from First Peter glided across him like a summer breeze. "Your beauty should not come from outward adornment, such as braided hair and the wearing of gold jewelry and fine clothes. Instead, it should be that of your inner self, the unfading beauty of a gentle and quiet spirit, which is of great worth in God's sight."

Jenni. She was that kind of woman. He'd struggled so long with his relationship to Tesha, wondering why he hadn't seen the truth before they'd married. They had been from two different worlds. At the time Todd remembered he'd drifted from his faith. Sunday mornings were often days to sleep in from partying the night before.

Tesha's life was glamourous and luxurious. How she looked and what she wore had been far more important than what she knew or thought, and much more important than how Todd felt about it all. He'd spent years feeling guilty, feeling he'd failed in the relationship without realizing why he'd failed—not that he didn't fit into Tesha's world but that he had never wanted his values to fit into her lifestyle. He knew in his heart something deeper was more important than a beautiful body and exquisite clothing. Morals and values, ethics and faith lasted. Beauty and style were fleeting.

Jenni on the other hand was true beauty—beauty of heart and spirit—as well as a good-looking woman. Todd glanced her way, admiring her sweet profile.

Instead of beating himself up for a failed relationship that ended in such tragedy, he needed to rejoice that, beneath his hardened spirit, God had not given up on him.

Somehow he longed for Jenni to realize how special she was and longed to touch Cory's life in a positive way. He'd made a start, and perhaps the Lord would continue to open windows until Todd could finally open the door of understanding and acceptance.

Todd glanced down at Cory fiddling beside him, and he slipped his fingers over the boy's hand and clasped it.

Cory tilted back his head, and his face brightened as radiantly as the sunlight that gleamed through the colorful stained-glass windows. With Jenni and Cory in his world, life had become color and light for Todd.

He lifted his eyes to the stained-glass picture of Christ. *Thank you,* he whispered silently.

Chapter Eleven

Todd stood beside Jenni in the candy shop and admired their masterpiece. He was confident they would meet their August deadline, and everything would be ready for the grand opening a week from Friday.

He looked up at the coral walls above the chair molding lined with walnut shelves filled with decorative boxes of chocolates—boxes the color of the walls with chocolate-brown script spelling out Loving Chocolate. Jenni had selected gold ribbon with a sprig of artificial bittersweet berries to adorn the packages. He had to admit it was perfect.

The counter and display cases were ready for business, and shelves lined the walls holding fancy cut-glass jars and tins to be used for candy containers. Below on a lower shelf, widemouthed jars of commercial candy waited to be scooped and weighed in bags or placed in the fancy containers. His idea, and perfect. He had some more ideas up his sleeve, but he'd contained them until Jenni was ready to listen.

Jenni insisted on selling stuffed animals, some fitted with elastic straps to which boxes of chocolates could be attached. He'd tried to sway her to sell flavored coffee beans, too, but she'd won that battle—a compromise, she called it—and they tabled the idea for later, too.

"Never thought we'd be ready to open on time," Jenni said.

"You haven't complained about the counter help I hired. I'm taking that as a good sign."

Jenni bumped him with her shoulder. "I never said all your ideas are bad. Hiring students from the community college works out well. They're responsible, I hope, and need money…just like us." She surprised him by encircling her arm around his waist as they stood side by side.

Their relationship had changed and grown. They'd become two people working in harmony…most of the time. They teased and he enjoyed the silliness for a change.

"Cory had a great time assembling those boxes," Todd said, gesturing to the stack lining the shelves. "I had to throw out a couple, but he tried."

"Since the fire, he's been trying to do better. I've complimented him, hoping he gets the point. It's an unending battle, but I'm hopeful one day I'll wake up and he'll be the same Cory he was when he was four."

"It'll happen." Todd slid his hand around her shoulder, their embrace bonding them together. Yet the nearness only reminded him of the hopelessness he felt. Jenni was still sending him the "no strings" message, not with words but with her actions.

Todd had to deal with his own stirred thoughts. He'd made a horrible misjudgment with Tesha. But Jenni? His heart told him his feelings were real and lasting. If only she would feel the same.

"I've been thinking about Cory. Since he's made such a valiant effort since the fire, I want to do something special for him."

"Like what?"

She sounded dubious, and he hoped she would agree. "I'd like to take him up north before school begins. Maybe as far as the Silver Lake sand dunes."

She sent him one of her looks that let him know she hated the idea. "We have the opening coming up." She looked thoughtful. "I suppose I can manage. We're in good shape except for—"

"No, Jenni. I want you to come, too. Look, if we leave on Saturday, we could come back Monday night or Tuesday morning at the latest. If we don't do it now, Cory will be in school and we'll be too busy."

Jenni gave him a one-shoulder shrug. "I don't

know. We'd really have to work hard those last three days."

"I know but it's our reward for a job well done."

Finally she gave him a halfhearted smile. "I suppose we can go. And Cory would love it."

Todd started to remind her he'd have to take the full-time position at Bay Breeze soon, but he stopped himself. Ian had indicated Philip would wait a while, but he feared Philip's patience would run out, and Todd didn't want to push his luck.

"By the way, I talked to Philip Somerville about the Hartmann party. Remember, Esther mentioned it?"

"I forgot about that. What do they have in mind?"

"The original plan was to celebrate the fiftieth anniversary of Loving Arms, but I guess the Hartmanns have decided to sell the house since the one sister's stroke and move to Cadillac to live near a niece. There's an assisted-living facility there where Abby will live."

"It's sad," Jenni said. "Loving Arms has been around for so long."

"Anyway, the party's September 17. They're hoping Abby will be able to attend."

"That would be nice," Jenni said, "but so sad."

Jenni surveyed the room again. Her gaze settled on the candy displays. She peered into the glass cases and struggled with a thought she hated to speak aloud.

"So what's swirling through that gray matter of yours?" Todd asked. "I can hear the bells ringing and cymbals clanging."

She sidled a look at him. "I hate to say it, but we'll need to come up with a bigger variety of chocolates one of these days, and something more creative than your bark or my clusters. Variety pleases people."

"I've been telling you that all along."

"I know, but I didn't want to rush things."

"You don't like to rush into things, do you?" His gaze locked with hers, and he brushed his finger across her cheek.

Her breath caught in her throat. "Rush into what?"

"New venture. New products." His finger drifted from her cheek and traveled along her jaw to her neck until he rested his hand on her shoulder.

Though their conversation was about candy, her thoughts had drifted back to something he'd said earlier, and she couldn't get the uneasy feeling from her mind.

Todd tightened his hand on her shoulder and shifted her toward him. "What's wrong? You look as if you've lost your best friend. Is it the Hartmanns' situation? I'm sorry. I didn't realize you'd feel so—"

She shook her head. "I'm fine." Jenni wanted to kick herself for letting her feelings show. She'd covered them for years, but lately Todd seemed to drag them out of her. Was it his tenderness perhaps or his curiosity? Whatever it was, something made her dig more deeply into the shadows of her memory.

"Just thinking," she added.

"About what?"

She hated his persistence. "About something you said."

He frowned, and she watched him search her face for a clue to his offense.

"It's not anything you said that upsets me. You made me think about—" She stopped herself. "Look, it's all in the past. Forget the past, right? We live for today and tomorrow. You said it yourself."

"But not if you're going to let it affect today." Todd clasped her arm and led her back into the kitchen. He pulled out a chair and settled it there, then sat across from her. "Jenni, I want to know about you. I see things in your eyes that I sense are hurting you, but you won't open up. I don't want to push you but—"

"Then stop. I don't want to talk about it."

"You're worrying me, Jenni. Is there something wrong?"

How could she lie to him? Her thoughts were a blend of things—her illness, her parents, Cory.

"Please." Todd looked at her with such sincerity she had to give him something. He'd told her about his marriage and about Ryan. He deserved something.

"I was thinking about my father," she said, giving him one small part of her sadness. She could see she'd captured Todd's interest.

"I've wanted to ask about him. Is he dead?"

"No."

"No?" He searched her face. "But you never talk about him. I assumed he'd died, too."

"He did, in here." She pressed her hand to her chest. Her father had been dead in her eyes long ago when he married Margaret and had turned his life over to alcohol, but mostly, when he'd rejected Cory.

Jenni told him the story of her hurt and anger, how she'd been alone when she needed family, how her father had destroyed her ability to follow the commandment to honor him.

"That was the worst," she said, thinking about the struggle she'd had to do God's will and failed. "I couldn't honor my father. He'd gone against everything our family believed in. He abandoned us and left us feeling as empty as when our mother died."

"She died young, didn't she?"

Jenni pressed her eyes closed to hold back the emotion wrought by her memories. "She was in her late thirties."

"That's so young. What did she die from?"

The words clogged in Jenni's throat, and she let only one escape. "Cancer."

"I'm so sorry," Todd said. "That's a horrible disease."

Jenni nodded, knowing too well how cancer could take a young life.

"Where is your father?"

She shrugged. "I have no idea. He and Margaret moved away and I was just as happy. I didn't have to run into him in town. He'd turned against Kris, and when she had Cory, he didn't want to be a grandfather. When she died, he came to the funeral—that was it—and he'd been drinking. It broke my heart."

"I suppose you have every right to desert him now," Todd said, "even though it hurts losing a parent."

"But the Bible tells us to honor our parents, and I know I should do something to heal the rift. I sense it, but I haven't been able to take action. I don't even know where to begin."

Todd stood and drew her upward and into his arms. "I understand how you must have felt all these years. Do you have other family members who can—"

"I have Cory. I've lost track of my mom's family. My dad was an only child. I don't have anyone to contact to find out where he is. It's just Cory and me."

"And me," Todd whispered into her hair.

Her heart lurched, wishing it could be true but knowing it could never be, no matter how much she wanted him. How could she offer herself to him as only half a woman?

* * *

Jenni stood at the bottom of the hill, looking upward at the giant mound of windswept sand. The late-afternoon sun beat off the dunes and shimmered on its surface, causing her to slip on sunglasses to mute the glare.

A shadowed silhouette waved to her from the top, and Jenni waved back at Todd standing at the pinnacle, waiting for Cory. When he appeared, the child's laughter pierced the air as he ran downward from the sandy rise until his feet slipped from under him. He sprawled downward, followed by a river of white crystals, his arms thrashing as Todd slipped and slid down the slope to keep up with him.

Jenni hurried to meet them near the bottom, grinning as Cory ran toward her covered with grit and a huge smile.

"Was that fun?" she asked.

He gave a huge head shake. "Come with us," Cory said, tugging at her arm.

"No way, Jose." She gave him a hug. "Todd's the brave one."

Cory tilted his head to send Todd a beaming grin. "We're the men."

"You sure are." Her heart tumbled just as Cory had on the dune. Todd had such a tremendous influence on him. Then sadness rolled in as quickly as her earlier joy. One day Todd could walk away, and where would that leave Cory? Where would it leave her?

Somehow, with God's help, things had to work out right.

"Ready for dinner?" Todd asked, resting his hand on Cory's light-brown hair. "We have a busy day tomorrow. The dune buggies and swimming."

"And more sand dunes?" Cory asked.

"And more sand dunes," Todd said, sending Jenni a tender smile.

Jenni's stomach tightened at Todd's sweet smile, but also at the reality. She realized she had to strengthen her faith. God could make anything work. The Lord could solve problems, and all she needed to do was ask for God's guidance and intervention. She had to trust, to know with assurance that God would not let her down this time. All things happened for a purpose, she'd told herself over and over. She truly couldn't wait to ask the Lord, face-to-face, why she'd had to struggle through so much.

One thing was sure. She'd come out stronger and more self-sufficient. If that had been the Lord's reason, He'd known what he was doing. The silly comment made her smile.

Todd smiled back as if he'd heard her thoughts. He stepped beside her and slipped his arm around her shoulder as they headed back to the car.

Dinner pleased Cory. They'd settled on a hamburger joint with greasy fries and thick juicy burgers. When Jenni noticed Cory's eyelids drooping and his eyes glazing over, she knew they needed to get back to the cabin before he fell asleep at the table.

"Too much fun," Todd said, tilting his head toward Cory.

The comment brought Cory into focus. "Tomorrow will be funner, I think."

"I'm sure it will be," Jenni said, feeling such deep love in her heart it almost hurt.

Todd paid the bill while Jenni steered Cory toward the car and the ride back to the rustic camping cabin where they'd left their gear. It had met their needs—two bedrooms with a living room kitchen and one bathroom. They figured they could share that without too much trouble.

They headed down Hazel Road and soon the park came into sight. They wended their way through camping trailers and finally reached the log cabins. Jenni grinned, recalling how Cory had asked if Abraham Lincoln had ever lived there.

By the time the car came to a stop, Cory was asleep. Todd carried the boy into Jenni's room and placed him on the cot.

"I'll let you get him ready for bed," he said. "Do you plan to turn in, too?"

She shook her head. "No, I want to unwind."

"Me, too. I'll see you in the living room." He caressed her arm and stepped through the doorway.

Todd stood in the center of the living-kitchen area and closed his eyes. He had no idea he would feel so drawn to Jenni and so fond of Cory. He really loved the boy who'd stolen his laptop, and lately he had a difficult time looking at Cory and remembering the angry child that he'd met that day on his front porch.

Todd shifted back and walked past the bathroom to his bedroom. He stepped inside and slipped off his boots and jeans. He needed to take them outside and pour the sand from all its secret hiding places. His sweatpants lay in a ball in the bottom of his duffel bag, and he pulled them out then slipped into them.

After making quick work of the unwanted grit, Todd settled on the sofa, hearing Jenni in the bedroom murmuring a simple tune to Cory who must have wakened. Though she wasn't Cory's biological mother, she had every attribute of a true mom. She defended the child despite his wrongdoings, she guided him with every skill she had and she loved him with all her heart. It was so evident. The scene touched Todd and sent an inner warmth coursing through him.

With no TV, he glanced around for something to occupy him while he waited—a magazine or even a pamphlet. He pulled open the drawer of a lamp table and spotted a red Bible. He'd seen them so often in motels, but never bothered to lift the cover.

Tonight was different, and he flipped open the book, letting his eyes focus where they were directed, not by him but by God. Todd halted at the book of Matthew, and he scanned the page. "Oh ye of little faith." The words jumped out at him. He'd had little faith as an adult and such accepting faith when he was a boy. He recalled God told people they must have the faith of a child. He prayed that the Holy Spirit opened his heart to understand what God had in mind for him.

He scanned the next words, realizing they had touched on his concerns. "For your heavenly Father knoweth that ye have need of all these things. But seek ye first the kingdom of God, and His righteousness; and all these things shall be added unto you. Take therefore no thought for the morrow: for the morrow shall take thought for the things of itself."

His head pulled back reading the last line. Stop worrying about things—what if this and what if that? Let God be in charge. Let God open his eyes to the truth. Todd realized he could never force Jenni to love him, but he could let God take over and allow the Lord full sway in his life.

He lowered the Bible into his lap and rested his head against the sofa cushion. Jenni's sweet song had ended, and his gaze drifted to the doorway. In a moment she stepped into the room, her feet nestled in slippers.

She grinned as she neared him. "I had so much sand in my shoes I could make my own dune."

"So did I," he said, telling her how he'd carried his clothing and shoes outside.

"What are you reading?" she asked, gesturing to the book in his lap.

He turned it over so she could read the cover. "The Bible."

"Really?" She gave him a surprised look.

"You've inspired me, Jenni. You've been through so much and still have such a strong faith."

"But not strong enough. Faith is like an acorn. Let it find roots in the Word and it grows into a mighty oak." She settled beside him and lifted the Bible from his hands. "Do you mind?"

"Not at all." He watched her slender fingers flick through the thin pages. She paused a moment, her gaze directed at the Scripture.

"Here's one of my favorite verses," she said. "It's in Psalms." She pointed to the verse. "'Weeping may endure for a night, but joy cometh in the morning.' Those words always fill me with hope."

His chest tightened, hearing her talk of hope and joy. He'd had so little of that in his life. "It's a wonderful Scripture, Jenni. Sometimes I forget when things are bad for a moment that tomorrow can bring a better day."

She returned the Bible, and Todd set it on the table, then shifted to draw Jenni into his arms. "It's been a nice day."

"And funner tomorrow," she said, making a silly face.

Seeing her relaxing and her face glowing sent Todd's heart on a spin, and he longed to kiss her.

Without resisting, Jenni nestled into his arms and rested her head on his shoulder. "Thanks for doing this for Cory. He's ecstatic. He drifted off, then woke again talking about tomorrow."

Tomorrow. The Bible verse washed over him. Don't worry about tomorrow. The sun will shine tomorrow. All good things come from the Lord. His heart filled with the assurance. Tonight he knew would be the beginning of something wonderful. "I'm crazy about Cory." He tilted forward and captured her chin in his hand. "And I'm crazy about you, Jenni."

She looked startled for a moment, then gave him a silly grin as if he were teasing. "You just like my chocolate."

"That, too," he said, longing for her to understand he was falling in love with her.

He sensed it coming and couldn't stop himself even if he wanted to. Jenni tilted her face upward, her eyes searching his while his pulse raced, knowing where he was headed.

It happened so naturally. She'd cuddled into his arms, then had lifted her full, parted lips upward in a gentle smile. Todd lowered his mouth, rejoicing that Jenni didn't pull away, but warmed to his embrace, wrapping her arms around him.

When her soft lips met his, Todd drew her closer.

Though he yearned to hold her forever, snug in his arms, discretion rose in his thoughts. *Don't scare her away.* He loosened his grasp and eased back. Her eyes were closed, and her lips looked tempting, but he grasped his heart by its strings and tethered it. *Slow and easy.* Mentally he repeated the words so they'd become his commandment.

When Jenni opened her heavy-lidded eyes, he saw concern in her expression. "I shouldn't have done that," she said.

"No, it was me, Jenni. I'm sorry." He faltered, having second thoughts. "No. I'm not sorry. I enjoyed every moment, but I don't want to upset you." He rested his hands on her shoulders, breathing in her fragrance and reliving the touch of her mouth to his. "We've shared so much the past few—"

"Don't apologize. We'll call it our once-in-a-lifetime kiss. How's that? No regrets."

Once-in-a-lifetime kiss. He couldn't believe what she'd said. How could he spend time with her, knowing the joy of her lips on his, and not want more? He shook his head. "Why? Why can't we be more than business partners, Jenni? I enjoy your company. Cory has come to mean so much to me. We've learned to fight our battles and come away friends. Why can't we let our relationship grow?"

Jenni lowered her head, her eyes downcast, and Todd couldn't imagine what thoughts raged inside her. He waited, longing for her to give him some reasonable explanation. He held back, hoping she'd say something, then with his patience waning, Todd cupped her chin and turned her face to his.

Her eyes had filled with tears, and his heart sank at the sight. "What is it?"

"It's impossible, Todd. I've been so afraid that this might happen. I've tried too hard not to let my heart overpower my reason."

His hand slipped from her chin as he grasped her shoulders. "But why? If your heart says yes, why fight it? I've been crazy about you for too long not to say anything. A person can only hide his feelings so long. Just be honest."

She didn't speak and avoided his eyes.

"You don't respect me, is that it?" Todd asked. "You don't like my personality? My character? Please, Jenni, give me some explanation."

A horrible shudder racked through her, then she lifted her head, her eyes so brooding, so hopeless, it broke his heart. "I have nothing to offer a man, Todd."

"What?"

"I have no idea what my future holds. I can't commit to a lifelong relationship when I don't know how long my life will last."

Disbelief tore at Todd's heart. "No one knows that, Jenni. I could drop dead tomorrow. I don't understand what you mean."

"Please, just accept what I'm telling you." She

drew in a rattling breath. "I've had a serious illness, Todd. My sister died and Cory became my responsibility while I was recovering. And so far so good. God's been on my side, but I never know. I live my life on faith. A weak faith, I know."

Questions tore through his head. Illness? Disease? He recalled her making some vague comment earlier. He'd assumed she had the flu or some common ailment. What illness? "Jenni, relationships are for better or worse. I'm willing to take my chances. Just tell me."

She lifted her head slowly, then her gaze captured his. "It's not that easy, Todd. I took after my mother, except I've been more lucky."

His heart spiraled in a downward plunge.

"I'm a cancer survivor."

His mouth fell open, but he found no words to express his feelings.

She rose and took a step away from him. "Don't say anything, Todd. I don't want your pity."

Chapter Twelve

Jenni tossed and turned in her sleep. She hadn't given Todd much chance to say anything. She'd excused herself and gone to bed while he sat with his mouth hanging open at her admission. Minutes later he'd called outside her door, but she'd whispered that Cory was sleeping and they'd talk in the morning.

But what did she have to say?

Shame filled her that she hadn't been more truthful. Her prognosis had been excellent, but she'd undergone surgery and treatment that may have affected her ability to have children. Why would a man want to take a chance with her? The disease had done too much to destroy her spirit for romance and marriage. She'd made the decision long ago. Her purpose in life was to raise Cory. That's all she needed. Nothing would change that.

Jenni trembled beneath the blankets, remembering Todd's kisses. She wanted to withdraw, to pull away, but she'd yielded to his gentle touch with her own. She'd been careless. She'd succumbed to emotion and let wisdom fall by the wayside.

Now in the darkness, longing ached within her. Todd had become a wonderful friend, a good business partner and, even more, a man she could love, but she would only disappoint him. She didn't want his pity, and that's what she saw in his face before she went to bed. She forced her mind to calm and finally she curled on her side, feeling sleep come.

Light seeped through the window, and Cory stirred. She glanced at her watch in the shaft of sun escaping past the shade. At 6:00 a.m. Jenni slipped her feet from beneath the blanket and arched her back to rise. She could shower and dress before Todd and Cory woke.

After grabbing her clothing, Jenni slipped from her bedroom and crossed to the bath. She peered at her bleary eyes in the mirror. She looked pitiful.

She turned the shower tap, and the water sprayed into the small cubicle. Steam began to rise and she stepped inside, letting the water wash away her self-pity and gloom. Today they planned to have fun with Cory. She'd block the events of last evening from her mind. She only hoped Todd could do the same.

When she turned off the water, she heard noises in the living area. Jenni dressed quickly, combed her hair and dusted her cheeks with a soft peach tint and daubed her lips with color. She drew in a lengthy breath before opening the door.

The first face she saw was Todd with eyes so full of sadness she wanted to weep. Jenni forced a smile. "Good morning."

He only nodded and gave a slight toss of his head toward Cory, drinking a small carton of orange juice.

"Ready for breakfast?" she asked Cory.

"Ready for swimming and the sand ride," he said.

"Dune buggy," Todd said.

The conversation seemed so stilted, Jenni wanted to forget the trip and go home. All she could do was pray that somehow the day provided them a time for healing.

Todd pulled into the dune ride's parking lot, listening to Cory chatter behind him. Breakfast had been miserable. He and Jenni had tried to act normal, but the whole event had been strained.

He'd barely slept last night, thinking of Jenni's announcement. Cancer. The word ripped through him like a knife, but what hurt him most had been her attitude. How could she have faith in God and allow herself to give up on life? She'd said it herself. She was a survivor. A survivor meant she existed. She was alive, but Jenni had condemned herself to half a life by fear.

He could hardly blame her. The word had jolted him. She'd mentioned her mother had died of cancer, but Jenni? He'd had no idea. What kind of cancer? He'd wanted to ask, but she seemed so sensitive, so reluctant to talk, he'd done the wise thing and not asked. One day she would tell him, and until that time, he would pray.

With Cory present, they had been unable to talk about last night, and Todd wanted the day to fly so he could express his feelings now that he'd had a chance to let her startling news settle into his mind.

"This is it," Todd said, nosing the car into a parking slot. "Be careful when you get out, Cory."

The boy unhooked his seat belt and was at Todd's door before he could open it. He climbed out, not trying to help Jenni. She'd gotten out nearly as quickly as Cory. The child slipped his hand into Todd's, and they made their way to the visitor's building so he could buy the tickets.

"What's going to happen?" Cory asked as they waited in line for a dune buggy.

Todd gave him a teasing poke. "Wait and see." He sidled closer to Jenni and brushed her arm. He feared she'd recoil, but she didn't.

"We need to talk," he said quietly, wishing they had some way to speak in code so Cory wouldn't notice or understand.

She motioned toward the child. "Not now, and what can either of us say?"

"I have a lot to say, Jenni." He rested his arm on her shoulder and gave it a squeeze. "What you told me makes no difference to me. None."

"That's because you don't understand," she said, her gaze shifting from him to Cory. "But thank you."

"Are you ready to have fun?"

"Sure," she said. "I've lived with the problem for years."

"I know," he said, wanting to kiss her and tell her everything would be all right. Instead, he slipped his arm around her back and drew her closer. He felt her stiffen, but she didn't pull away, and that was a good sign.

Their dune buggy rolled forward—a roofless Jeep body with four wide seats behind the driver protected by a roll bar. "Climb aboard," the driver said, helping them into their seats and assisting with seat belts.

When the eleven passengers had crowded in and buckled up, the driver climbed into the buggy, then headed across a narrow wooden bridge that led them toward the giant sand dunes. Like a herd of reclining multihumped camels, one dune rose after another.

As soon as they hit the Sahara-like scene, the driver stepped on the gas, and the buggy bounced and jolted up one dune and flew down the other. Cory's laughter split the air, and even Jenni smiled as the wind tangled her hair. Grains of crystal rose as the Jeep surged forward and swirled on the wind before it settled on Todd's skin and gritted in his mouth.

"Look!" Jenni cried as they charged to the summit of a towering dune.

Todd looked in the direction where she pointed and spotted the glistening water of Lake Michigan. Sailboats split through the waves and seagulls looped and squawked overhead above the noise of the buggy's motor.

Disbelieving, Todd realized they were heading for the beach and the lake. As they shot down the sand toward the lake, Cory grabbed his arm, his giggles exploding in the roar of wind and motor. They hit the beach with a bounce and headed for the water.

Jenni let out a gleeful cry as the Jeep zoomed into the surf with the spray rising above them sprinkling them with water. Veering back to solid ground, the driver braked, and the buggy skidded to a stop. "Climb out if you want to wade," the driver called. "We'll be here fifteen minutes."

Cory was the first to tug off his shoes and step into the water. He cringed at the cold and called out that it was too icy. Todd and Jenni moved in closer, both disinterested in wading but wanting to keep a close eye on the child.

When Todd turned to Jenni, she shook her head. "Tonight, okay? Let's just enjoy the day."

She'd read his mind. Questions bounded through him as wild as the dune buggy ride, sending gritty thoughts and fears through him. He would wait until tonight, but it would be one of the hardest things he'd ever done.

Jenni settled into a canvas chair at the camping park's pool. Cory decided the lake water was too cold and opted for swimming at the park. Todd played with him in the water while Jenni sat in the sun hoping to dry her suit. She knew Todd would corner her soon, and she needed to think of what she could say to help him understand she cared about him more than anyone except Cory, but she couldn't get involved in a relationship. Too much hurt. Too much disappointment.

The sun sent a warmth washing over Jenni as she watched Todd steer Cory to the shallow part of the pool. Todd was genuine and caring, a wonderful person. Jenni watched him give Cory instructions, then climb the three steps to the pool's deck.

When he reached her, Todd grabbed a towel and rubbed it over his hair, then dried his body. Since they'd met in the early spring, the summer sun had tanned Todd's skin, now leaving him with a bronzed glow that gave him a healthy, vigorous look. How could she not find him appealing?

He sank beside her in a chair and stretched out his legs to the warming rays. "Nice, isn't it?"

"Very, and Cory's having a blast."

He leveled his eyes to hers. "And we're not?"

"I didn't say that. We're both thoughtful."

Todd reached across the distance and brushed his fingers along her arm. The sensation sent a ruffle of yearning into her chest. She wanted to cuddle to his side and forget the past, but she stayed seated, frozen to the horror of what had been and the fear of what might be.

"I'll talk fast," Todd said, "because I'm sure Cory will be here in a minute, but I want you to know that I don't fear the past, Jenni. I can only imagine the nightmare of your illness and the difficulty of having your sister die at the same time. That's why you're so strong and so confident."

"But I'm not," she said.

"You're stronger than you think, and that's why I believe you're shortchanging yourself."

She opened her mouth, but he stopped her.

"Because of what the future could hold, you've stopped looking ahead—not for the business or Cory, but for yourself. You're giving up your own happiness for a 'what if.' What's happened to your faith? You know God can do anything." He searched her eyes. "You deserve something wonderful in your future, Jenni. All I'm asking is you think about it. Give us a chance."

Seeing his sincere face sent an ache so deep into Jenni's heart, she could hardly breathe. What could she say to dissuade him? "It's so complex, Todd."

"Only to you, Jenni." He scooted his chair closer.

"Look at Tesha. She was gorgeous, she had a glamourous career, she had money and material things, and she had good health, her whole life ahead of her—not even an illness that I can recall besides a cold. But her life ended in her prime. She didn't expect it. It happened."

Tesha was gorgeous. If he only understood that was part of the problem. "I know" was all she could say.

"You've been given a second chance by God's grace. You're still here, and you have Cory. If nothing more, Jenni, he needs you to live. Don't give up on living it to the fullest. Cory's lost too much. He can't lose you, so you have to live, and God wouldn't do that to the boy. He wouldn't."

His tone was so vehement that Jenni glanced around to see if anyone heard him. No one seemed to. What Todd had said smacked around inside her head. If she died, if anything happened to her, Cory had no one. Todd was right about that.

But that wasn't the whole point. Jenni had much more to tell him if she could, and she couldn't. She couldn't bear his pity.

"Jenni?"

"I'm thinking," she said, lifting her distracted eyes to his serious face. If she could only enjoy his company and his tender ovations without fearing a commitment. Todd had never mentioned marriage. He'd only mentioned their growing friendship.

Could she let her fear go? Could she accept his embrace and his kisses without worrying about what if he asked her to marry him?

"You've made a good point, Todd. I talk about faith, but where is mine?"

"Don't chastise yourself. We all trip ourselves up and fall. Then we need a friend to pick us up. I'm making that offer."

"And I'm accepting," she said. "Be patient, Todd. It's a big change for me."

"I have the patience of a saint."

She laughed. "Since when?"

"A minute ago," he said, slipping his fingers through hers.

His strong hands enveloped hers, and she sent up a silent prayer for courage and wisdom. God had an answer, and she needed to hear it.

Jenni pressed her foot on the brake and squealed to a stop at the red light. Her thoughts had been tangled in the letter she'd received after she'd arrived home from the store the day before. It seemed uncanny that she'd been speaking of her father recently, and yesterday a letter from him had arrived.

She'd had a difficult time opening the envelope, and when she had, the contents had torn at her emotions.

She'd hoped that life would finally smooth out. The grand opening had been a success. Friends, established customers and new ones had dropped by to enjoy candy samples, drink pots of coffee and even make purchases. They'd had a few unexpected orders, and Todd had set appointments with a couple of resorts to make the candy available in their establishments. She couldn't have asked for more.

Since they'd returned from Silver Lake, Jenni had watched Todd's interaction with her, looking for signs of pity or despair. She'd seen none. He treated her the same as before she'd told him about her cancer. The fact amazed her.

With the store's success and new orders coming in, Jenni had too much work to do, and now her father wanted to see her. The light changed to green, and Jenni forced her mind to focus on the traffic.

Jenni made her way and pulled into the parking lot behind the store. She climbed from the car and gathered the bags of groceries from her trunk. Earlier she'd called Todd to say she'd be late, and now she prayed he hadn't done anything ridiculous. She never knew what might happen when she left him alone in the kitchen with his creative thoughts. Her heart lifted at the thought of Todd. He'd become her right hand in so many ways.

Before she opened the back door, strange sounds erupted from the interior as if Todd were being serenaded by an unmusical steel drum band. She pushed open the door and stepped inside, then came to a careening halt.

Todd darted across the kitchen wielding a large metal spoon, his head helmeted by a stainless-steel pot. Though the vision confounded her, his ballet was more than comical.

"What are you doing?" she yelled as he pirouetted past her.

He thrust the spoon forward, banging it against the range hood, then twirled around and darted off again. "A bat!"

A bat? Her first thought was a baseball bat, but before the idea settled, a flying mouse soared into her thoughts. "You mean a real bat? With wings?"

"Yes," he bellowed, doing another sashay past her.

Jenni couldn't tear her gaze from his gyrations. His broad shoulders and muscled arms flexed, wielding the spoon as he flitted by, but the cooking pot helmet was more than she could handle. Laughter sputtered from her throat. She set the groceries on the counter, then grabbed her closest defense, a cardboard box, flung it over her hair, and joined him with a spatula.

Finally, the flying varmint sailed into her line of vision, and she brandished her utensil with no avail. Then, like two soldiers flushing out the enemy, she flailed the spatula from one side of the room while Todd flourished his spoon from the other, and the poor winged rodent didn't know which way to turn.

With one wide swing, Todd smacked the bat like

a baseball. It shot across the room, fell to the floor and lay unmoving near the back door. Todd darted across the tile, dropped a newspaper over the tiny beast and scooped up the critter.

"Don't hurt it," Jenni yelled, startled by the compassion she felt for the pitiful creature. "Just put it outside."

Todd gaped at her. "What?"

"You know. Be gentle."

"Be gentle? You sure you don't want me to take it to a vet?" He rolled his eyes.

"Don't be ridiculous. Just put it outside somewhere. Away from our door. Even a bat deserves a chance."

Todd shook his head and disappeared through the back exit while she waited, wrapped in thoughts. *Even a bat deserves a chance.* The reality struck her cold. Her father. She hadn't been willing to give him a second chance.

Finally the back door swung open, and Todd returned, empty-handed. "Done," he said. He stepped beside her and slipped his arm around her shoulder. "You're such a softy. I laid him next to the trash bin. If he flies away before next Thursday, he's saved. Alive and forgiven."

Forgiven. She hadn't given her father the same opportunity. She wasn't a softy. She'd been heartless and unloving. The pain flooded her, and she felt as if she were drowning.

Chapter Thirteen

Todd jolted when he heard his words. *Alive and forgiven.* He'd spent so much time not forgiving himself for Ryan's death and not loving Tesha as he'd vowed that he hadn't felt alive for years. Jenni, too—she'd stopped living, afraid that her life might end too soon. The paradox seemed overwhelming.

Todd's thoughts flew back to his Sunday school days. He'd learned that Jesus loved him and all he had to do was open his arms to the Lord and accept the gift, but as he grew older, he'd become unbelieving. It seemed too simple.

Yet sitting in church with Jenni had brought him back to those years when he'd accepted the Bible with the faith of a child. One story stood out in his mind—the ailing woman who'd touched Jesus's hem. Christ had said to her, "Your faith has healed you. Go in peace and be freed."

The words settled into his mind like a recurring song he'd learned years earlier. If not for God's loving pardon, his life would be as useless as that bat's, but the Lord, in His compassion, lifted him up and carried him to safety, forgiven and freed?

"You didn't hear me." Jenni's voice snapped him back to the present.

"I'm sorry." He drew closer to her shoulder. "I was lying out back with the bat. What were you saying?"

"I was telling you about a letter—" She spun around and sniffed the air. "I smell something burning."

"Burning!" His eyes widened, and he bolted across the room. "The chocolate."

"Chocolate?" She followed him. "What were you doing?" She charged to the stove and jerked the pan off the burner. "Todd, you can't put chocolate directly on the heat."

"How am I supposed to know?"

"You're not. I'm the candy maker." She grasped two nested pans and shoved them toward him. "This is a double boiler. You melt chocolate over warm water. Look at all the chocolate you wasted."

He whiffed the acrid odor and felt as rotten as the smell. "Maybe we can salvage it."

"No one likes scorched chocolate. It permeates the batch. This is garbage."

"I thought I'd get started to please you."

To please her. Jenni's defenses crumbled when she heard his excuse. Like a slapstick movie, the whole pitiful situation raced through her head, and she laughed. "I'm sorry for yelling. I guess your intentions were good."

He laughed with her as she crumbled into his arms, and when his arms pinioned her to his chest, she caught her breath, realizing she'd lost the battle with her emotions. Jenni eased from his embrace not because she wanted to, but because she knew it was best.

Todd's dimples flickered in his wry grin. "I suppose I need to listen to you for a change and let you make the chocolate."

She loosened her grasp and her hands slid down his arms. "What we really need is for you to learn to make the chocolate correctly. I'm going to need your help as this business grows, and one day I might be gone, and you'll have to carry on."

"Gone? Please, Jenni, you're not talking about—"

She lifted her finger to his lips, shushing him. "No, not that, but things happen."

"What kind of things?" He eyed her suspiciously.

"I was trying to tell you about it." She'd wanted to push it from her mind, but the letter had roused her emotions and tangled her in confusion.

He'd captured her finger and kissed it before lowering her hand, but he continued to clasp it in his. "Tell me. I'm listening."

"Remember how we talked about my father so much recently?"

"Yes," he said, searching her eyes.

"I got a letter from him. Him or Margaret, I wasn't certain. It was signed 'Dad' but it was done on a computer."

"Amazing," he said, "and after so many years."

Jenni nodded, but she considered the event more bewildering than amazing.

"What did he say?"

Her pulse kicked as she thought about the letter. "He's very ill. Emphysema." She shrugged. "From smoking, I suppose. His lungs are gone. He doesn't have long to live."

"Then you'll want to see him," Todd said, so matter-of-factly it threw Jenni a curve.

"I don't want to see him, Todd. That's the problem."

"But—"

"I know." She felt tears well in her eyes, tears of guilt and sadness. "The Bible tells me to forgive and to show compassion. I just showed a bat more compassion than I want to show my father. It makes me feel horrible, unworthy, rotten."

"Oh, Jenni." He drew her back into his arms. "The bat didn't hurt you. It was only a nuisance. Your father injured you greatly when you needed him. It's natural to feel the way you do, but you can't treat him as he treated you or you're no better than he is."

"Maybe I'm not any better. Maybe it's genetic." She'd said the words just to say them, but the truth struck her. Maybe it was in her blood to be vindictive.

"You're wrong. Let the letter settle in. Give your shock a chance to resolve, and you'll see I'm right. You'll never forgive yourself if you don't go."

She turned away, unable to respond. Todd had been correct. Forgive so you can be forgiven. Hadn't she read that over and over in the Bible? What would the Lord think of her hard-hearted stance on her relationship with her father. "Honor your father and your mother, so that you may live long in the land the LORD your God is giving you."

"Give it a couple days, Jenni, but don't wait too long. He could be writing to you from his deathbed. You don't know how much time you have."

Todd's words grated in her ears. Why had her father written now? *Lord, help me find compassion and forgiveness. Help me to follow Your commandment to honor my father.*

"I told Ian I'd start full-time the first of the year," Todd said, as he filled a carton with miniature boxes of candy for the Hartmann party. He gave Jenni a glance to see how she'd taken the news.

"Waiting won't put your position in jeopardy, will it?" Jenni asked.

Her concern sent a warm sensation jogging up his

arms. "No, he understands." He folded the lid on the carton and grabbed another. "Philip's thoughts are focused on the party right now, so I'm safe for a while."

She smiled at him, then went back to stirring the chocolate in the double boiler.

So much had happened in the past month. The business had grown weekly until they now wondered if Jenni would be able to keep up with the candy orders. To Todd's delight, the bark he'd accidently created had become popular, and it was easy to make in the large sheets—even he could handle that—but Jenni's kisses with the flavored chocolate were a favorite.

Cory had gone back to school. Fourth grade. So far so good with his behavior. The attention Todd had given the child and Jenni's freed-up time had been what the boy needed. He wasn't demanding. The child just wanted to be reassured he was loved and wanted. Todd had no doubt that Jenni adored the boy.

The lack of progress fell in two areas: Jennie's visit to her father and her relationship with Todd. Both caused an ache in Todd's chest.

Jenni had been his date at Dale Levin's wedding to Bev. He'd felt so good with her at his side. People had begun to think of them as a couple, and so had he. If only Jenni would. He let the thought fade.

Todd had been amazed how easily it had been to attend worship again. After he'd been going a few weeks, he realized he'd been yearning for something to fill his emptiness. Though a relationship with Jenni would also make him more complete, God's Word had given him a sense of wholeness and eased his loneliness.

Jenni and Cory did that, too.

"Why so quiet?" Jenni asked from the counter where she was unmolding kisses.

"Thinking," he said. "It was nice that Philip invited us to the Hartmann party. I don't know the ladies, but so many people will be there. It's almost the event of the season."

"I know. Esther said these ladies have touched the lives of so many people. It should be interesting. I've been thinking, too."

He paused and turned to look at her. The sound of her voice gave him concern. "What about?" He hoped the topic was her father.

"The shop," she said. "I'm afraid I'm going to have to hire someone to work back here with me. The front help's working out well. They seem conscientious, and so far, the cash register balances."

"That's good news." Todd left his cartons and crossed to her side, chuckling. "Come here." He used his index finger to beckon to her.

"What?"

He repeated the motion until she left her chocolate and faced him.

"I know that's difficult for you, and I'm proud of

you. If you want this business to grow, there's no way you can keep this place stocked alone, especially once I'm working full-time."

She lowered her head and gazed at the floor. "I know. It's just difficult. I need someone I can trust, and someone who knows her way around a kitchen."

"I like the *her* part."

She lifted her gaze and frowned.

"I don't want you hanging around in here with a man."

She smiled, and a sweet sensation rolled through Todd. He bent down and kissed the end of her nose. To his pleasure, she kissed him back and then added a couple of Eskimo kisses, the nose rubs making him smile.

"My chocolate's cooling," she said. "I know you're right, but I have to wait until I can't do it anymore, and then I have to find the perfect person."

He took a chance. "I always thought I was the perfect person for you, Jenni."

She didn't smile, but put a hand on each side of his face. "You are," she said as her face washed in an appalling sadness that threw Todd off course again.

What could he do to help her see what she was doing? He'd never met a woman so bent on self-sacrifice as Jenni, and he prayed one day he'd understand.

* * *

Jenni flipped the pages of a magazine, waiting for her appointment at the Loving Hair Salon. She needed a cut badly and decided to get it styled before the Hartmann party. She wanted to look her best since she never knew when she might meet a potential client. Though she'd been pleased having Todd take over the promotion, Jenni missed the relationship with outside buyers and the public.

The partnership with Todd had been more than Jenni could have ever imagined. Not only had he become an excellent business promoter, but he'd changed her. For years—forever, it seemed—she'd been on her own with Cory, carrying the burdens of mothering and bringing in wages. She'd had no one she could lean on except a few friends, and Jenni wasn't the type to ask friends for help.

If she'd told people her struggles, her newfound church family would have been at her door. The thought made her realize she'd never told Todd that she'd also slipped from her faith when times were bad. She believed in God's love and mercy, but she thought the Lord had decided she wasn't worth the bother. But in her most desperate moments, in the pit of despair, she cried out and God touched her heart. Since that day, she'd read her Bible and had attended church again.

Another blessing came when Todd began to attend worship with her. Whether she'd initiated his action or not, she knew the greatest work was the Holy Spirit who'd opened Todd's heart to listen and accept God's promises. The event gave her joy, but it frightened her, too. Faith was another way she and Todd had bonded. Each supported the other in focusing on where to put their faltering trust. They were both guilty.

Jenni couldn't help but think of Tesha. Todd had said little about his marriage, and part of her wanted to know about his life with a gorgeous model. The other part had avoided asking. As soon as the thought crossed her mind, envy rose like a wraith, filling her with doubt and insecurity.

"Jenni."

She pulled her gaze from the blurred magazine article and placed it back on the rack before walking to the stylist's station. "I'm ready," she said.

"Great." She pointed to the young woman waiting at a sink. "Hannah will shampoo your hair."

Jenni slid into the reclining chair in front of the basin. The young woman named Hannah gave her a shy smile as she opened the thick towel. Jenni's gaze was drawn to a series of large bruises on the woman's arm, and when she studied her face, she noticed a bruise on her cheek, which she'd tried to cover with makeup.

"How did you get the bruises?" Jenni asked quietly, realizing she was being nosy, but she felt concerned.

"I fell," the woman mumbled as she wrapped the towel, then a cape, around Jenni's neck and shoulders.

"Lean back," Hannah said, gathering Jenni's hair and holding it up while she rested her neck on the rounded support of the washbasin.

"You have thick hair and such a pretty color," Hannah said as she added the coconut-scented shampoo.

Jenni thanked her while the aroma wrapped around Jenni's senses. She closed her eyes, letting the curiosity of Hannah's bruises drift away while her own concerns settled over her.

Once again her father's request to visit weighed on her mind. Why couldn't she dismiss the letter from her mind or give in and go to see him? Resentment knotted in her chest while, at the same time, God's Word filled her. Not long ago, she'd opened the book of Kings and was startled at the scripture that caught her attention. "And he did evil in the sight of the LORD, and walked in the way of his father, and in the way of his mother."

Jenni feared this is what she had set herself to do. Her father had ignored her need when she was sick and when Kris had died. He'd abandoned her at a time of great need. Jenni's decision had been to follow the Old Testament view, an eye for an eye and a tooth for a tooth.

But Jenni knew that Jesus had said to turn the

other cheek, to treat others as you wanted to be treated. She felt pulled in both directions until her body and mind ached from the tugging.

"Are you a regular customer?" Hannah asked.

Jenni opened her eyes, surprised to hear the woman's question. "I'm usually only in for a cut, but today I'm going for the works."

"A special occasion?" Hannah asked.

"We're going to a party at Bay Breeze. I own Loving Chocolate, and we're providing favors for the event."

"You own Loving Chocolate." Her voice had an admiring ring. "I love your kisses."

The warm water rinsed through Jenni's hair until Hannah turned off the tap and stepped in front of her with a clean towel. Her eyes sparkled. "I used to make chocolates. I had molds, and sometimes I even made truffles. The ones without alcohol."

"Really?" Jenni's interest piqued with the woman's excitement. "Why did you stop?"

Her face paled, and she gave a one-shouldered shrug. "Life gets complicated sometimes."

"That's too bad. I started making candy as a hobby. Suddenly it grew into a business. I had no idea it would happen."

"You're so blessed. Candy making's one thing I know how to do well," she said, as if someone had convinced her she didn't know much at all.

"Would you consider going into the business?" Jenni's heart kicked with the rising thought.

"I'd drop this job in a minute," she whispered with a stifled grin. She pulled the towel away. "You're ready," she said, gesturing toward the stylist.

"What's your full name?" Jenni asked.

She looked uneasy for a minute. "Hannah Currey. Why?"

Jenni smiled. "You never know when I'll need to add staff to my shop. I'll keep you in mind." She gave the woman a wave and headed across the room, feeling as if the Lord had once again given her direction. She erased the worry from her mind. *Thank You, Lord,* she said to herself.

Chapter Fourteen

Jenni gazed through the wide windows of the Bay Breeze Restaurant that looked onto the rolling waters of Lake Michigan. The afternoon sun glinted on the ruffled waves like tiny mirrors bobbing on a sea of turquoise.

Little by little, the large restaurant had begun to fill with familiar and unfamiliar faces. On each table, Jenni and Todd had placed a display of miniboxes of chocolates for each guest—not only a thoughtful gesture, but great advertising for the shop.

Todd stood across the room, talking to someone Jenni didn't know, and she took the time to admire him from afar. Today he wore a dark navy suit with a pale blue shirt and navy print tie, but he'd become more handsome since the day she met him. Now she knew the man inside the suit. His good looks couldn't compare to his kind, compassionate nature and his playful wit.

Jenni's heart ached. She wanted so badly to open her arms to him, to strip away the facade and fear that surrounded her and let Todd face the truth she'd hidden. No matter how hard she tried, glamourous Tesha rose in Jenni's thoughts.

Todd turned her way, and Jenni shifted her gaze to Jemma Somerville. She'd worked so hard to make this a special, yet sad, going-away party for the elderly sisters.

Todd reached her side and captured her hand. "We just made a nice sale. Details at eleven."

She laughed at his TV-reporter delivery. "I can't wait. Who's the man with Philip Somerville? They resemble each other, but I've never seen him."

Todd shrugged. "I don't know, but I'm sure we'll find out."

Though Jenni felt somewhat out of place, not knowing the Hartmanns personally, she had been pleased to be invited. Rarely did she have a chance to dress up and attend a social function. And the bonus was, Cory didn't whine when going to the sitter's.

She watched as Philip ambled from group to group across the room. No pretension there, Jenni thought. For a wealthy man, he looked and acted no different than anyone else.

"Nice job on the candy," Ian said, reaching their side of the room with his wife.

Jenni thanked him and greeted Esther as the conversation drifted to the weather and the party. Within minutes, Jenni glanced across the room as Philip headed their way with the good-looking stranger. She studied the two men as they approached, and guessed the man had to be a relative. The similarity was uncanny.

"Thank you for doing such a nice job on the candy," Philip said to Jenni, then shifted his gaze to include Todd. "I'd like you to meet my brother, Andrew. He's just arrived back in Loving, to our delighted surprise."

Andrew clasped each person's hand with a firm shake, yet seemed uncomfortable at his brother's comments.

"You've been away a long time?" Jenni asked.

"For more years than I can count," he said.

"Too long." Philip slipped his arm around his brother's shoulder. "It's wonderful to have him home again." He gave Andrew's shoulder a squeeze. "This means another party for—"

"For his prodigal brother," Andrew said, finishing the sentence. "It's more than good to be home and to be so welcomed, but I keep telling him to forget the party."

Philip chuckled. "No such luck. We want to kill the fatted calf for this next shindig."

Jenni sensed an unspoken dialogue going on between the brothers, but for once, she didn't let her inquiring mind ask the question. She had a difficult time imagining the handsome Andrew as a true prodigal son, but then, she'd learned everyone had their secrets.

Philip and Andrew moved on, and Jenni couldn't stop herself. "Ian, what was that about?"

Todd subtly elbowed her, as if validating that she was out of line for asking. Ian gave a half grin. "Andrew was the black sheep. He took part of the family fortune and left to make his own way in the world. He didn't do well from what I've heard, and his leaving didn't set well with his father or Philip. I don't think he came back when his father died. It's been one of those quiet rumors that Philip avoids talking about. I sense a lot of hurt."

Jenni felt ashamed. "Thanks. I shouldn't have asked."

Todd chuckled. "You can say that again," he whispered.

Ian shook his head as if to relieve her from her uneasy feeling.

A waiter came around with fluted glasses filled with sparkling juice for a toast, and the room hushed as Philip moved toward a microphone. Someone clinked a piece of silverware against a piece of stemware, and the voices faded to a murmur, then hushed.

"Thank you all for coming," Philip said. "Today we're celebrating and also, sadly, saying goodbye. Abigail—Abby—and Silva—Sissy to most of us—

have been blessed with fifty years of being hostesses and owners of the Loving Arms Bed-and-Breakfast."

A murmur rose in the room, and Jenni grinned when she overheard someone say it was a rooming house, but the sisters liked the sound of a B and B better.

"Sadly, Sissy and Abby have decided to leave our fair city and move closer to relatives due to Abby's health."

Jenni noticed the two women hovering close to Philip, one wheelchair-bound and the other as sprightly as a canary. She wore a yellow dress with a multihued fringed shawl that Jenni guessed had come from Claire Dupre's Loving Treasures boutique.

"The Hartmann sisters' love for the community will not leave us," Philip said. "The Loving Arms name will remain on the building since the sisters have graciously taken a financial loss so their home can become a shelter for abused women."

Applause resounded throughout the room, and Jenni's mind shot back to Hannah at the hair salon and her suspicion.

"I'd like to propose a toast for God's blessings on Abby and Sissy as they settle into their new lives in Cadillac, Michigan. They will never be forgotten."

Glasses were lifted and people took a sip, followed by cries of "Here, here." Sissy moved to Philip's side and accepted the microphone.

"Thank you," she said, her voice quaking with age and emotion. "You have all been like family to me and Abby. We've shared your joys and sorrow. We've laughed with you and cried with you. We will miss you all, but God has led us to realize that moving to be closer to our niece would be wise. We accept God's bidding."

Murmurs rose from the people, cheering them and acknowledging what Sissy had said. The word *family* settled over Jenni like a weight, arousing too many unwanted thoughts.

Sissy turned again to the crowd. "God has given us many gifts, and besides our Lord's death and resurrection, the greatest is love. You have been that gift to us. You have been family and friend. We have touched each other's lives with faith and forgiveness, and we want to thank you from the bottom of our hearts. The Lord be with you all and be gracious to you. May His love shine on you, in good times and bad, and give you peace."

As people hurried forward to hug the two women, Todd's gaze shifted to Jenni. She looked unbelievably beautiful today. She wore a pale-green dress with white trim that flattered her shapely figure. He'd noticed her gray eyes looked almost green. Her thick flowing hair had been harnessed in a clip and fell in soft tendrils to her neck.

But when he looked closer, Todd spotted tears in her eyes, then watched them roll down her cheeks.

His heart lurched as he wondered if they were tears for the sisters or for herself. His chest tightened as he touched her arm and drew her away from the other guests to the windows.

"What's wrong?" he asked, lifting his finger to brush away the moisture from her eyes. "This can't be over the sisters."

"Partly," she said, turning to face the window.

"And the other part?" He slid his arm around her waist and felt her tremble.

"Me," she said. "Sissy talked about family and love, and I know I'd allowed my heart to harden against my father."

He could have said I told you so, but that wasn't what she needed to hear. Jenni had learned this for herself, and that was important.

"Family." Jenni brushed the back of her hand against her cheek. "My dad is all I have except Cory. How could I let an opportunity God has given me pass?"

"You're right," Todd said, caressing her bare arm.

"Healing is what I need. We've created such a deep chasm between us, and now God has given us a chance to bridge the gap."

"What will you do?" Todd asked, praying he knew her answer.

"I've decided to take God's offer. I'll visit my father as soon as I can arrange it."

Todd lifted his eyes heavenward, sensing that

until Jenni had rid herself of the past she would never be ready for the future. "I'm so happy. That's what I wanted to hear."

She sent him a faint smile. "The business and Cory—I have so many things to think about."

"Where does your dad live?"

"Not that far," she said. "I was surprised. He's in Michigan. In Fennville. It's below Holland off of U.S. 31."

"I'll watch Cory for you. Don't worry about that."

"I know you will," she said. "What would I do without you?"

Her words washed over him sweeter than the chocolate she made. He'd do anything for Jenni if she'd only let him.

Jenni's mind had been so preoccupied with visiting her father, she'd forgotten to tell Todd about Hannah. Since Jenni had met her, Hannah had also lingered in her thoughts for two reasons—the possibility of hiring her for the shop and the concern Jenni had for the woman's bruises.

Since she'd faced the truth, all she could think about was her own unyielding sin. A Bible verse she'd heard in church a couple of weeks ago gnawed at her thoughts. "And he walked in all the sins of his father, which he had done before him: and his heart was not perfect with the LORD his God, as the heart of David his father." The scripture didn't make her think of her father, but of herself. She'd walked in the same footsteps as her father, and her heart was far from perfect. The need to be forgiven cried out to her as loudly as the need to forgive.

The road signs blurred past as Jenni drove toward Fennville, blending with the trees, some of which were already changing color in the September weather. She'd already passed through the city of Holland and had connected with Interstate 96. Deciding to drive to her father's on Thursday had been wise. So far, the traffic had been light, and she hoped it would be light on her return.

Todd had come through, as always. He'd agreed to pick up Cory from school, and if need be, he'd keep Cory overnight, but Jenni planned to return home later in the evening. She saw no reason to stay once she'd spoken with her father.

Cory had filled her thoughts, along with feelings of regret. Why hadn't she adopted Cory? He seemed so much like her own child. It wasn't too late, she reminded herself.

As she neared her destination, Jenni felt tension mount. How long had it been since she'd spoken with her father? Five years had passed since Kris's funeral, but she could hardly count that day. Her father had walked in and out with no fanfare. Margaret clung to his side, and Jenni wondered facetiously if the woman were bolstering him from having drunk too much alcohol.

Jenni's attitude had been bad and still was, she feared. Fighting her negative feelings, she turned her thoughts to God's Word, knowing only the Lord could ease her worries and give her courage to do the right thing. "If any one of you is without sin, let him be the first to throw a stone." The message stabbed through her mind and heart.

She'd been sinful more than she could count, so why should she judge her father? Was one sin worse than another? The only sin that came to mind was the sin of rejecting the Holy Spirit, and even then, with repentance, God opened His merciful arms. *Lord, be with me,* she pleaded. *Guide my actions and words so I don't behave in a way that will offend and make things worse.*

Margaret slipped into Jenni's mind, and she clamped her jaw to hold back the anger that charged through her. She needed to stop blaming her stepmother. She had no idea what was in Margaret's heart. Her prayers rose as she followed the signs into town.

Her father had included his telephone number in the letter, and Jenni had found the strength to call. Margaret had answered and given her directions, and now she followed them as best she could. Her hands gripped the steering wheel, her tension rising.

Finally she read the street name and turned, breathing a relieved sigh. When Jenni spotted the house number, she pulled to the curb. Her pulse escalated, leaving her dizzy and addled. She shifted into Park and sat, willing her heartbeat to slow, and praying she would get a grip on herself.

She'd come with nothing—no gift, no flowers, only herself. Anything different would have seemed a lie. Today the meeting was not social, but one of healing. Jenni pushed open the car door and stepped onto the concrete street. She grabbed her handbag, closed the door and locked it, then made her way to the porch.

As she approached, she realized the residence was a duplex. She checked the addresses beside each door, then pressed the right bell. She waited. No sounds came from inside. She tried the bell again. When no one answered, Jenni reverted to knocking.

Irritation spiked inside her, overshadowing her nervousness. She'd told Margaret she was coming today. Why would the woman not answer the door? Sabotage?

"Hello," she called against the silent barricade. A shudder ran through her, followed by the feeling of dire hopelessness. *Lord, why is this happening?* Why had her father asked her to come, then refused to see her?

Frustration and hurt pierced her, remembering the abandonment she'd felt years ago so like the emotions she was feeling now. How could she have allowed herself to be duped again into trusting, into expecting honesty and concern from her father when he had none when she needed him?

Jenni spun on her heel and stomped across the porch to the stairs. As her foot lowered to the first step, she heard the sound of a door opening. Her heart rose to her throat, and she pivoted as disappointment overwhelmed her.

"Who are you lookin' for?" the woman asked from the next duplex doorway.

"My fa—Mr. Anderson. He was expecting me, and—"

"They took him away," the woman said, scrutinizing her. "Are you the daughter?"

Jenni's head spun while her lungs knotted, cutting off her breath. A whisper escaped. "Yes."

"The EMS took him about an hour ago."

Jenni searched the woman's face. "Was he—"

"Dead?" She shook her head. "Not that I could tell."

"Any idea where they would take him?" Jenni's hands quivered as she slid her purse higher on her shoulder.

"My guess, to Holland Community Hospital. It's the closest. About twelve miles from here."

Apprehension and fear weighted Jenni's shoulders. "Could you tell me how to get there?"

"Just go into Holland, and it's on Michigan Avenue and Twenty-first Street. You can't miss it."

"Thank you," Jenni mumbled, stepping backward and wondering if the woman really knew where her father had gone—twelve miles back, and what if she were wrong?

The day before, Margaret had said Jenni's father was about the same, not well but no worse. She'd assumed she'd find her father home.

Jenni headed to her car, stunned by the turn of events. The stress settled in her temples, and her head pounded as she made her way back to U.S. 31.

Memories invaded her as she turned her car toward Holland. As a child, Jenni had clung to her father, knowing he was her protector and provider. Though she saw his weakness as she grew older, he had loved her mother and stood by her side until her death. Jenni had expected her dad to grieve, just as she and Kris had mourned their mother's loss so deeply, but he'd startled them.

When Margaret walked into their home just two months later, Jenni had asked herself how her dad's behavior could be construed as grieving. Today as she hurried to see him, Jenni tried to understand. Had Margaret been a balm for his grief? Had her father been so blinded by sadness that he didn't realize so little time had passed? Or had his life been so happy with her mother that her father couldn't imagine living without a woman in his life?

Judging. Jenni winced, realizing she'd been sitting in judgment. God had warned people about judging others. He alone knew what was in a person's heart. The lesson had been difficult, and Jenni still ached, remembering her loneliness and depression when she'd faced her own cancer and her sister's death without support. She could barely deal with even the remembrance of the anguish and bitterness she'd felt toward the world and the Lord. How could a merciful God strike her with two blows at one time?

Self-pity could destroy healing, Jenni admitted. She had clung to it too long, living in the past and longing for it to change.

The past? Todd had said it, and it was true—the only thing she could change was today and the future. Jenni gazed ahead of her, watching the sun flicker like a strobe light through the trees against her car hood. *Heavenly Father, help me release the past. Give me strength to face today and courage to change tomorrow, according to Your will. In Jesus's precious name. Amen.*

Jenni rolled her shoulders, willing the tension to ease away. Billboards advertised motels and local attractions in Holland, and in twenty minutes, Jenni pulled into a gas station for directions to the hospital.

She followed the station attendant's instruction to Washington, then headed north. Soon she could see the hospital jutting above the surrounding buildings. Her heart rose to her throat again, knowing that her father might not have come here at all, and she had traveled all this way without an opportunity to resolve anything.

An unwanted thought rose in her mind. Her father could be dead. The concept sent sorrow through her while she prayed the Lord would offer her this chance to repent and forgive.

Jenni pulled into the hospital parking lot and made her way to the information desk. Relief washed over her when the woman called the emergency room and stated her father was there. After making her way through the corridors, she stepped into the emergency area and identified herself.

"I'm sorry," the nurse said. "You'll have to wait. He's still with the doctors."

He's alive, Jenni thought. Yet her anxiety to see him made her fight frustration. Was God trying to tell her something? She'd sensed the Lord had led her here, but no matter which way she turned, she felt blocked.

"Please sit in the waiting room with your mother, and we'll let you know when you can go in."

Her mother? The words stabbed her. Jenni opened her mouth to rebut, but closed it again. She pictured Margaret alone. "Thank you," Jenni said, and turned in the direction the woman had pointed.

Her heels clicked on the tile floor and joined the ringing in Jenni's ears. *Todd, I need you.* The thought settled over her, kicking up her pulse. Todd. Her protector, her solace. She could turn to him with her problems. Without him, life seemed too empty and too lonely.

When Jenni stepped through the waiting room door, she spotted Margaret. The woman's face looked gaunt and ashen. Her hair straggled beside her thin face, adding to her haggard look. Pity rose in Jenni's heart as she headed toward her.

"Margaret." She stood above the woman. "Are you okay?"

The woman lifted her tearstained face as a look of relief washed over her. "Hello, Jenni. I'm very worried, but I'm glad you came."

"How is my father?"

She gave a slow wag of her head as she motioned to the chair beside her. "He's fighting for his life. I'm sorry I couldn't call. It all happened so fast, and I figured you were already on your way."

Jenni only nodded, searching the woman's face for answers. "What happened?" She settled into the chair beside her.

"It's his lungs. They're failing. I'm sure that wanting to see you has kept him struggling to make it." Her voice rasped with years of smoking.

"Wanting to see me?" Jenni's voice faded, letting the meaning wash over her and drowning her in emotion.

"He's a changed man. He quit smoking, something I haven't been able to do, but it's too late for him. A year ago he pulled out an old Bible. He's been too sick to read it, so he asked me to read to him and we've prayed that you would come to see him. He was ashamed, Jenni. Too ashamed to come to you—he feared your rejection."

Nausea rose to Jenni's throat. Prayer. Had she ever prayed for her father? Had she ever asked the Lord to reunite them, to heal the chasm between them? Shame mixed with sorrow filled Jenni so quickly, her tears erupted into heart-wrenching sobs. She put her face in her hands and wept for what might have been if she had prayed years ago, instead of despised.

Rather than seeking healing, Jenni had allowed the pain to swell and grow into a different kind of cancer that ate at her soul rather than her body. *Lord, forgive me.*

Jenni turned to Margaret, brushing the tears from her cheeks and seeing her stepmother's eyes bear testament to the love she held for Jenni's father. "Forgive me for not trying to make amends sooner. I was deeply hurt. I felt so abandoned."

"Shush," Margaret said. "Your father had been very wrong. We've both been wrong. You and Kris reminded him too much of your mother. He'd tried to bury all of you to escape the heartache. He made a horrible mistake, and it took him years to face what he'd done to alienate himself from you."

Jenni reached across the distance and touched the woman's frail arm. "The important thing is I'm here now, and I'm praying God gives me time to talk with him."

"He will, Jenni," she said with such assuredness, Jenni's skin prickled. "Your father's waited too long for this moment."

"Is he going to—"

"Only God can answer that," Margaret said. "We've been through this before. Maybe not today or tomorrow." Her head swung in a slow rhythm. "Whatever time is left, we'll make the best of it."

She covered her mouth and released a hacking cough that roused Jenni's pity, but she realized that each person has his or her own addiction, not always tobacco, drugs or alcohol, but sometimes an addiction to some other self-indulgent need. Jenni's had let her dependence cling to the past, to intemperance and to an old sorrow. She'd been as guilty as her father.

"Mrs. Anderson."

They looked up as the nurse approached them and beckoned. "He's ready now."

"You go ahead," Margaret said. "I'll give you some time alone."

Jenni studied her face. "Are you sure?"

"Positive."

"Thank you," she said, rising. She bent down and kissed Margaret's cheek. The action surprised her as well as Margaret.

Her stepmother's face pinched with emotion. "Thank you," she said, her eyes glazing with tears.

Jenny caught her breath and pressed her hand against her chest to stem her emotion. Her legs trembled as she took her first step toward her father.

Chapter Fifteen

Jenni turned and followed the nurse down the corridor, then through the double doors into the emergency room. Cubicles lined each side, and the woman pointed. "He's in number three."

Though her feet pushed her forward, Jenni's anxiety held her back. She forced herself to move and took a lengthy breath before pushing back the curtain. When she stepped inside, tears slipped from her eyes and rolled down her face.

In front of her lay her father, his skin gray and sunken, connected to oxygen and an IV drip. Monitors measured his heart rate and blood pressure while oxygen was being measured by a clamp around his finger. He didn't move, but as she stepped forward fighting her emotions, her father's eyes blinked.

"Daddy?" she said, hearing the alien word leave her mouth.

He tugged his glazed eyes open and looked at her. "Jenni?"

She nodded, disbelieving that this frail man had once been her protector. "Margaret told me to come in first. She'll be along in a minute."

His hand shifted toward her, and Jenni placed her palm over his fingers, feeling icy flesh beneath.

"I'm sorry you're having problems," she said.

He labored to speak, and she tried to quiet him. He needed rest, not an emotional setback. "I'm sorry…for everything."

His hushed, breathy words touched her ear like a feather.

Jenni patted his hands. "Don't try to talk. I understand."

His head shifted as if he still wanted to explain, but he failed, and he let his cheek fall against the pillow.

"The important thing now," Jenni said, "is we're here. And even more important, God is here." Jenni knew that with all her heart. She felt the bitterness drain away from her body, replaced by sorrow for years they'd both lost.

"Cory?" The child's name left his lips as a whisper.

"He's okay." No, Cory was better than okay now, and the remembrance filled her with joy. Todd had come into her life and with it, Cory had changed just as she and Todd had. "He's great, Dad. He's almost nine and in the fourth grade. He reminds me of Kris."

A faint smile curved along her father's mouth. "A good boy." His eyes sought hers.

"He's had his moments, Dad, but he's doing fine now. He's smart. He loves electronic games." Todd's laptop shot into her thoughts. "He even knows a little about computers." She gave a silent chuckle. That laptop had caused a miracle. *Thank You, Lord, for all Your surprising gifts.* Because of that laptop, she'd met Todd, and Todd had influenced Cory's behavior, then had touched her life. "I'll bring Cory next time I visit."

"Next time." Tears rimmed her father's eyes, and when they shifted, Jenni followed the direction. His hand lifted an inch, and she realized he was gesturing to the Bible that lay on the bed table.

"Do you want me to get your Bible?" Jenni asked.

He gave a single nod.

She withdrew the Bible and noticed a folded piece of paper used as a bookmark. When she studied the paper, she read 1 John 1: 8–9. "Do you want me to read this?" She showed him the note.

"Please," he mouthed, unable to speak.

She located the verse and scanned the words, her chest tightening with awareness.

"Read," he rasped.

Jenni didn't know if she had the courage to read aloud the Scripture that summarized their lives. She cleared her throat and willed the words to come. "If we claim to be without sin, we deceive ourselves and the truth is not in us. If we confess our sins, He is faithful and just and will forgive us our sins and purify us from all unrighteousness."

"Forgive me, Jenni." Each word seemed to drag from her father's chest.

"Forgive *me,* Daddy." She grasped his fingers and bent low to kiss his limp hand.

No more words needed to be said. Healing came like a morning sunrise. Though days might be cloudy or rain might fall, beneath the gloom Jenni knew the promise. "Weeping may endure for a night, but joy cometh in the morning." Today was her joy.

She and her father were reunited at last.

"Time for bed, Cory," Todd said, shaking the child who'd fallen asleep on the sofa, concerned about his schoolwork.

Cory sat up in a daze and looked at him through heavy-lidded eyes.

"Did you finish your homework?" Todd asked, gesturing at a textbook lying on the floor. He lifted the book and glanced at the open page. "The Legend of the Petoskey Stone," he read. "See this?" Todd pointed to the photograph.

The boy looked at the page, then at Todd. "That's a Potsky Stone. It's from Michigan."

"It is," Todd said, grinning at the child's mispronunciation. "I have one around here somewhere. I'll look for it and you can take it to school."

"Really?"

"Sure thing. Now let's get you up to bed."

Todd followed Cory up the stairs, and in moments, he tucked the child into bed and turned out the light. He stood a moment, watching the boy curl into a ball and remembering him having so much fun helping at the store after school. Cory had grown since Todd had first met them, both in size and in behavior. The angry, sullen child who was heading for real trouble had done a one-hundred-and-eighty-degree turn.

Thank You, Lord, for that, Todd thought for the millionth time, as he went back downstairs. God had given him a chance to atone, a chance to do something right. Todd had messed up with Ryan, but he'd been blessed with this gift, the chance to help Cory…and Jenni.

On the phone, Jenni had shared the details of meeting her father, and with each revelation, Todd rejoiced, knowing his prayers had been more than answered. He assured her he'd take Cory to school in the morning and pick him up from school after his work at Bay Breeze. The clerks were handling the store, and the good help eased their minds. He also reminded her that Cory was in good hands. In loving hands, if she only knew. The boy meant too much to Todd now. If Jenni didn't give up her foolish notion that a relationship was out of the question, Todd didn't know what he'd do.

Cancer. The word made him boil. Why Jenni? She'd endured so much. Why had the Lord caused her to suffer more? Todd realized he would never know, but out of the suffering, Jenni had strengthened and learned patience. She had developed courage and confidence…except when it came to love.

Todd sank into the living room chair. He knew cancer could return. Yet over five years had passed since Jenni's surgery, he'd calculated, and so far, to his knowledge, she'd remained cancer free. What was Jenni's prognosis? He wondered if she had some secret knowledge she hadn't shared, or was it only her fear?

Spurred by his thoughts, Todd rose and grasped his laptop. He plugged it into the outlet and connected a nearby phone line, then tapped the on button. He settled back into his chair, watching the computer desktop open, then clicked to the Internet.

In moments, he'd typed "cancer" into a search engine. The site connected, and he scrolled down looking at the overwhelming choices. He would be there all night. He clicked on a medical site and scanned the information, hitting links and reading.

Diagnosis, prognosis, treatment. Type? He had no idea what type of cancer Jenni had. She'd never said, and he'd been too afraid to ask. She was so sensitive, and he'd realized that even telling him about her cancer had devastated her. He felt lost not knowing.

Ovarian, uterine, breast, lung—each had its own prognosis and various treatments. He let the knowledge seep into his mind, then compiled it, organized it, because he needed to know. "Oh, Jenni," he whispered. "Tell me what I'm fighting so I know what to do."

His plea became a prayer. He'd come to realize that his relationship with Jenni had long passed the friendship stage. He wanted more, and he prayed one day Jenni would, too.

Jenni heard the store's back door open and saw Todd step into the kitchen. As if they belonged together, he hurried to her side and wrapped his arm around her shoulder, drawing her to his side. His gaze drifted across her face as if he were memorizing each line. "I missed you."

"Me, too. You were on my mind."

"I'm glad." He lowered his mouth to hers, his lips awakening the longing she'd had to open her heart and take her chances.

Her senses awakened to what could have been… to what might be. His hand brushed along her shoulder, then captured her chin, deepening the kiss. When he eased back, Jenni drew in the sent of autumn clinging to his skin. She ran her fingers along his hairline, feeling the thick dark strands beneath her hands.

He nuzzled her neck, his lips whispering against

her ticklish skin. "I dropped Cory off at the sitter's. I told him I'd pick him up in a couple of hours."

She squirmed away, trying to contain her grin. "Thanks," she said, overwhelmed by the sensation of belonging that blanketed her.

"Tell me what happened," Todd said, pulling out a chair and sitting on it backward, his hands resting on the chair back.

She told him the full story, her improved kinship with Margaret, the Scripture she and her father had shared and the forgiveness they'd given and received. "I can't change what happened," Jenni said, "but I can let it go. I should have done that years ago."

"We've all made that mistake, Jenni. I've lived for years blaming myself for my brother's death. I wallowed in the guilt and allowed it to affect my life. Why had I held it to me like a prize rather than a burden?"

"But that was different, and now you know that you weren't to blame."

"No. I still believe I could have made a difference, but I've let it go. It's too late to change it now. All I can do is use the experience to do better next time. That's what you've done with your father."

"He doesn't have long," Jenni said, facing the reality that made her ache. "Time is short, and I want to see him again. I want him to meet Cory."

"You can do that. I'll help you all I can."

She closed the distance between them and rested

her hand on his. "I know. It'll be different…and difficult, when you're working full-time."

He raised his other hand and clasped it around hers. "We'll adjust, and by then you'll have some help. We'll find someone to—"

"Oh, I forgot to tell you about that," Jenni said, telling him about meeting Hannah at the hair salon.

"She sounds like a perfect answer," Todd said, lifting her hand and kissing her palm. "Things work out. They just take time."

Jenni had grown to know Todd well, and now as she looked in his eyes, she realized his sentence had more meaning than talking about Hannah.

"We need to talk tonight, Jenni," he said, her fingers still close to his lips. "I'll come over after Cory's asleep and we'll—"

"Come for dinner," Jenni said. The urgency in his voice set her on edge, but Jenni had needs of her own. No matter what Todd wanted to say, tonight she needed to share the truth about her cancer.

"Bring Lady along, too. The dog will wear Cory out." She sent him a halfhearted grin, having made her decision. The time had arrived to let her heart heal or let it break.

Todd handed Cory the dog brush. "Please be gentle."

Cory sat on the ground with Lady squirming in front of him. "Like this?" he asked, trying to keep the dog in one place while tugging the brush through her tangled locks.

"Firm, but gentle. Lady needs a good brushing to get the knots out."

Lady wiggled free and gave Cory's face a wet kiss while the boy giggled.

"I can't," Cory said. "She won't lay still." His eyes widened as if some great truth had struck him. "But Lady's a good dog, isn't she?"

"Sure. She's tops," Todd said, trying to read the boy's thoughts.

"You won't send her back to the humane place ever, will you?"

"Never." Todd finally understood the fear. "When a dog's lovable, like you are, no one would ever send it anywhere."

Cory thought a moment, then patted the ground and waited. Lady wagged her tail with a flourish, her tongue panting for attention. The child tapped the ground again, then grinned when Lady curled up beside him.

Cory drew the brush through her hair, then looked at Todd with one eye half-closed to block the sharp rays of the setting sun. "Am I lovable?"

"You know you are. Are you worried about that?" Todd asked, realizing the depth of Cory's thoughts.

"Not anymore, I guess, but I used to be."

Todd knelt beside Cory and placed his arm around the child's shoulder. "Even then, when you were having lots of problems, your aunt Jenni would never have sent you away. She loved you too much."

"Like God?" Cory asked.

"What do you mean?"

"Even when we're bad enough for Hell, he still loves us and forgives us so we can go to Heaven."

"I guess you could say that," Todd said, stifling a grin. "But God's love is much deeper than any human's. Still, your aunt Jenni comes in a close second."

"And you're third?"

"I'm nose to nose with your aunt Jenni."

Cory's face brightened as a smile blossomed. "I love you."

The child's admission wrapped around Todd's heart. "I love you, too, pal. I always will."

He rose and stood beside the child, watching him a moment as he tackled brushing Lady's hair. Emotion rolled across him like tires of an eighteen-wheeler. Tonight he would lay the truth on the table. He needed to know where he stood with Jenni. If she pushed him away, too many people would be hurt, including Cory. The child had lost so much already. If Todd had realized months earlier where his feelings were leading him, he might have backed off. "Might have" was the key. Cory became his mission early on, and Jenni became his dream.

Watching, he slipped his hand into his pocket and felt the Petoskey Stone he'd brought from home to give Cory. He'd promised to find it, and he figured the child might enjoy seeing the unique ancient coral fossil found along Lake Michigan, but he let the stone alone. Why distract the child from his task with Lady? There was always later.

Todd turned away from the scene and stepped inside the house, his nerves fraying as he realized tonight could be the beginning or the ending of his relationship with Jenni.

The scent of dinner met him in the back hall and guided him into the kitchen. Jenni turned when he came through the doorway, her face thoughtful.

"Dinner's almost ready," she said.

He strolled behind her and slipped his arms around her waist and lowered his lips to her bare neck. Tendrils of hair like feathers brushed his cheek. "You're beautiful, Jenni."

"Thanks, but you're exaggerating," she said, glancing over her shoulder.

"You're beautiful to me," he whispered into her hair.

Jenni's back stiffened, and she edged away, then turned. "How can you even suggest such a thing? You were married to a model. That's beautiful."

Todd's pulse bolted. "You're wrong. She was glamourous on the outside. Beautiful is different."

"Right." Her tone sounded facetious as she returned to the stove.

"I'm not trying to start an argument. Tesha was

rail thin, and for all the beauty on the outside, I learned too quickly it was missing on the inside."

Jenni pivoted. "You were married to her, Todd. You must have found her appealing. Why would you say this now if not to make me feel better?"

Todd didn't understand what she meant. Why was he trying to make her feel better? Better about what? But he could enlighten her, he knew. "I don't talk about Tesha much, Jenni, not because I treasure her memory but because I'm ashamed at how shallow I was not to see it sooner."

"What are you talking about?" Her voice rose with irritation.

"I won't deny it one bit. When I first saw Tesha, and when she started playing up to me, I was knocked off my feet. Someone that glamourous was actually flirting with me. I reveled in telling people I was dating a model. For a while I became her groupie. I followed her from one modeling gig to another, making sure everyone realized I was with the striking woman, but after we married, soon, I learned that her values and mine didn't go anywhere. She wanted luxury, and I wanted a life—a house, a family, an occasional quiet evening."

Todd's pulse escalated as he watched Jenni's face flicker with disbelief and then dismay. "Tesha was a party girl, alcohol, sometimes drugs—something I didn't believe in—but she said she needed them to keep going. By the time I realized that I'd made a horrible misjudgment, it was too late."

"But you loved her," Jenni said.

"Yes. Once I did, but that ended long before her death."

"You stayed married to her."

"I didn't know what else to do. I'd made an oath and I never believed in divorce even though my faith was in the pits. I knew what God expected, and divorce seemed like a failure."

"I'm sorry," Jenni said. "I didn't know."

"I should have told you. That's why I've always been careful about relationships. This time I have to do it right and not get swayed by the wrong things."

The wrong things. Jenni's mind raced to Cory. Todd had gotten tangled in their lives because of Cory. Though Todd's kisses seemed real, Jenni often wondered if the attraction for her had really been for her nephew.

"But I'm stronger now, Jenni," Todd said. "I know the difference between infatuation and commitment."

"Do you really think so? Can't we all be duped by our emotions?" What had her own feelings been? What were they now? She couldn't face the truth.

"I don't think I can be duped anymore." Todd pressed his hand against his chest. "I know what's in here, and that's what I want to talk about."

Jenni's heart skipped a beat, and she opened her

mouth to stop him, to tell him that the dinner was ready, but before she could act, Lady came tearing into the kitchen with Cory on his tail.

"I'm hungry," he said. "And so is Lady."

Jenni glanced at Todd and saw disappointment register on his face.

"Later," he said.

She nodded, wanting to forget the conversation because she knew that tonight would end a beautiful friendship. It could go no other way.

"Wash your hands for dinner, Cory," she said.

Jenni turned away, hiding the tears that welled in her eyes. She closed her eyelids to squeeze back the emotion, and her heart squeezed back.

It was all for the best. It was the only way.

Chapter Sixteen

Jenni brushed strands of hair away from her cheek as she came through the doorway into the living room.

"Is he sleeping?" Todd asked.

"Finally." She'd been frustrated tonight. Cory was as wound up as a top, and her mission sat on her shoulders like a two-ton truck.

Lady perked up her ears and pattered across the room to sniff Jenni's legs. Then giving her a haughty gaze, she lifted her nose and ambled into the hallway, probably heading for Cory's bed, Jenni figured.

Jenni headed across the room and sank into a chair, then curled her legs beneath her. The time had come to face the truth. Todd had indicated he had things to say, and so did she.

Todd beckoned to her. "Sit beside me," he said

with an anxious look. "You're a mile away over there."

She shook her head. "I'm comfortable here."

A frown replaced his puzzled expression, but Jenni knew she needed to keep her distance. She felt too out of control, and she needed to quit hiding the anguish she felt. Once he knew more about her cancer, he'd finally become her silent business partner. The kisses and romantic gestures would end, leaving Jenni lonely yet knowing she'd done the right thing.

"What's on your mind, Jenni?" Todd shifted uneasily on the sofa. "I mentioned earlier today that we needed to talk, but now I sense you're avoiding me. You've distanced yourself, and I don't know why."

"I could lie and say everything is fine, but it isn't, Todd. I know you wanted to talk about something, so why not tell me. What's this about?"

"Us."

"Business?"

"No. Us. You and me. Our relationship."

"Then that's business, because that's what our relationship should have stayed."

He arched his back away from the seat cushion and leaned closer. "What are you telling me?"

Her heart constricted, and she felt her breath leave her. "I'm afraid you want to talk about you and me having a romantic relationship."

"Why are you afraid? You know I'm crazy about you."

Jenni grasped her courage. "I figured as much. I've begun to feel the same, Todd, but I already told you that I'm not up for a real romance."

"I want to go beyond romance, Jenni. I think we have something special here. I love you."

"No, you love Cory."

His face blanched, and his head drooped. "I can't believe you would say that." She heard him sigh before he looked at her. "I love Cory, yes, but I love you. I want to make plans. I want—"

"It doesn't matter what you want. This is what must be. I'm not putting myself or anyone through a relationship that's a guessing game."

Todd's voice blasted from her chest. "Guessing game? You're not making any sense."

She slapped her hand against her chest. "Me, Todd. I'm the guessing game. I already told you I had cancer once. That's a sentence to a life of guessing. I have no guarantees that I can't have a recurrence. I can't put you or anyone through a lifetime of uncertainty. It's hard enough for me."

"Let me be the judge of what I can handle, Jenni."

His pleading look broke her heart.

"After you told me," Todd said, "I went online and read everything I could find on cancer. I know you have no guarantees, but neither does anyone. I could walk outside and get hit by a truck. I could fall down the basement stairs and break my neck. No one has guarantees."

"This isn't a wager where we pick odds, Todd. I have a greater chance of dying because of the cancer. I survived it once, but can I do it again?"

"Oh, Jenni." He lowered his head and wagged it as if in defeat.

"Todd, please, let it go. If I were ever going to get involved with anyone, it would be you. You're wonderful, and Cory loves you."

"And you love me," he said, his head rising like an arrow and his gaze pinning her to her chair. "You love me, so why can't we have faith that God will keep you safe? You're a woman filled with faith. I don't understand."

She drew up her shoulders at his persistence. Why couldn't he accept what she said or get angry and walk away, slamming the door? Instead, he studied her face as if waiting for her stony heart to soften and change. "It's more than that, Todd. Much more."

"Try me. What is it?"

"During my treatment, I had to take medication that suppresses the ovaries. Then I took another one that stops a woman from being childbearing. You deserve to have children, and I have no guarantees that I can."

He rose and knelt beside her. "Look, Jenni. I read about that in the research. Lots of women have children after they've used those medications. If God decides you can't have children, you have Cory. He's been a gift in so many ways. You must believe me."

"What if I'm pregnant and the cancer returns? Treatment could endanger the fetus."

He grasped her hands. "I read about that, too. Women have had those experiences. Women who've been through cancer treatment can give birth to normal, healthy babies. You're talking about fear, Jenni, not reality."

Jenni jerked her hands free. "I'm talking about breast cancer, Todd. I've had a total mastectomy. How can you find that beautiful?" She leaned forward, her eyes narrowed and filled with anguish.

Her bitter words stabbed Todd's heart. Breast cancer. The reality washed over him like a torrent.

"You see," she said. "That makes a difference. I've been mutilated. I'm only half a woman."

Todd's chest ached from the pent-up emotion. He looked at Jenni, remembering her sweet face with wisps of hair brushing her cheek, her eyes filled with hope, but today they were filled with desperation, the same desperation Todd felt. How could he make her understand?

Todd rose, his eyes searching hers. "I didn't fall in love with your body, Jenni. I love all of you, everything about you—your lovely face, your red hair, your smile, your mind, your humor, your spirit. I can't separate the parts from the wholeness of you. Do you understand?"

"You've never seen it, Todd. I can barely look at it myself. I have nothing. No evidence that I was a woman. Skin stretched over bone, that's all I am there."

"If it would make you feel better, they do reconstructive surgery, and—"

"Silicone or saline isn't a substitute for real tissue."

"Jenni. I'm sorry." Todd regretted the suggestion. His voice knotted, and he struggled to release the words that poured through him. "I wish I could change things. I wish I could heal you, not your scars, but the sadness."

"I cried, Todd. When it happened, I cried and cried some more, not for the loss of my breast, but from the loss of my life as I knew it. Nothing will ever be the same. I've avoided romance and any hope of love, because if it weren't part of my life, I didn't have to deal with the loss, with the scars, the evidence."

Todd was at a loss for words. A Bible verse nudged in his thoughts, but even that, it seemed, wouldn't be enough to sway Jenni. "People touched the hem of Jesus's garments and were healed, Jenni. They went away rejoicing. Let's rejoice that you're alive. You've been cancer free for five or more years."

"After I went through it all as well as Kris's death and having Cory come to live with me, sometimes I thought I could hear God's hushed voice telling me I'd get through it all and be better for it. That didn't happen."

"Yes, it did," Todd said, remembering the hours they'd spent together before this revelation. "You're strong and courageous. You're organized and have perseverance. That's why you've shocked me with all of this today." He knelt again beside her, a question building in his head. "Why didn't you tell me this before?"

"Because I knew you'd walk away."

"You don't see me moving, do you? I'm here for the long haul, Jenni. Let's take the journey together."

"I don't want you to see me this way. I can't do it."

Todd grasped her hands. "Tell me you don't love me, Jenni, because that's the only way I'll leave you." Her look stabbed his heart.

"I don't love you," she said, her voice quaking with sorrow. "You're free to go."

Frustration, then anger, ripped through Todd's being. He rose, his eyes searching hers. He knew what she'd said wasn't the truth.

His hands sank into his pockets, and he touched the Petoskey Stone he'd planned to give Cory. He rubbed his fingers over the smooth, polished surface, then pulled it out. He eyed the unique pattern—the evidence of minute coral cells now as empty as his heart.

He reached out and pressed the stone into her hand. "One day I'll tell you the legend behind this stone, but for now, I'd like you to have it."

"It's a Petoskey Stone," she said, eyeing the rock.

"It was once a thriving colony of living coral, Jenni. Today it's dead, a fossil without life. It's only a trinket, a souvenir of what once was." He stepped back, unable to handle the loss he felt. "Think about that, Jenni. It was once living and now it's dead. When you look at this stone, remember this promise. I will love you always."

He willed his legs to move, to carry him from her house, to walk away without turning back.

"Where's Todd?" Cory asked, hanging on Jenni's chair. "He hasn't been here for a week."

"I told you. He's busy."

"I miss him." Cory twisted around and slid onto the chair arm.

So do I, Jenni thought. She opened her hand and gazed at the Petoskey Stone; its intricate honeycomb pattern glowed in the lamplight.

"What's that?" Cory hung over her lap and stared at the rock.

"It's a stone."

"Can I see it?" Cory asked.

She dropped it into his hand, and he slid his fingers over the shiny surface.

"Todd said he had a Potsky Stone for me, too."

"Petoskey," she corrected. "They're found on the beaches of Lake Michigan and Lake Huron. They're special."

Cory held the stone close to his eye and studied the design. "I have a story about it in my schoolbook. That's why Todd said he'd give me one."

A story? Could he mean the legend Todd had mentioned? "Do you remember the story?"

He shook his head. "It's in my science book."

She shifted in the chair and peered at the stone. "Could you bring the book home tomorrow?"

"It's in my room. I'll get it."

Jenni waited, wondering what Todd had meant about the legend. Todd. He filled her thoughts every moment since she'd sent him away a week ago. He'd called, and she'd been abrupt. He'd come to the store, but she'd kept it all business. He looked so dejected, and she felt the same. Empty. Lonely. Incomplete.

Part of her wanted to believe that Todd wouldn't be repulsed by what he saw, but she had been. She hadn't been prepared for the result even though she'd been told. Breast. Gone. Little left to reflect her womanhood, but she had lived. Todd had reminded her of that. She was alive to care for Cory and to build her chocolate business and to laugh at Todd's silliness…except Todd was gone.

She'd sent him away.

"Here it is," Cory called, bouncing across the carpet with the book balanced on his head with the help of his hands. He swung it down and dropped it in her lap.

She flipped open the pages and finally checked the index. Petoskey Stone. She saw the reference and turned to the page. A vivid picture of the stone headed the brief story of the legend. Jenni scanned the story.

A French nobleman and fur trader named Antoine Carre married an Ottawa Indian princess. Soon he was adopted by the tribe and made chief, and one night his wife bore a son. In the morning, Carre saw the sunlight shining on his son's face, and he named the child *Petosegay,* translated to "rising sun" or "sunbeams of promise."

Sunbeams of promise. Todd had left her with a promise—*I will love you always.* Tears rose in Jenni's eyes, and she brushed them away so Cory didn't notice. "Thank you," she said, handing back the book.

He returned her stone and skipped off to his room with the book.

Jenni rubbed the smooth stone between her fingers, her heart aching with confusion. Why couldn't she release her fears? Her favorite verse rose in her thoughts. How could she not believe that's what the Lord wanted for her. "Weeping may endure for a night, but joy cometh in the morning."

Did she want to live in the darkness or bask in the sunbeams of Todd's promise?

Jenni raised her hand and brushed it against her chest, not feeling the scar, but knowing it was there. Would she allow her wounds to destroy her life?

Would she allow her pride to ruin Cory's chance for a wonderful man in his life?

She pressed her palm against her chest, feeling the anguish in her heart.

Heavenly Father, help me to rise above the scars that not only mar my body but my spirit. Show me how to accept the sunbeams of promises. In Jesus's precious name. Amen.

Jenni rose and headed for the telephone. She wouldn't blame Todd if he hung up on her, but she wanted to tell him how sorry she was. She wanted to ask for another chance.

Todd couldn't believe Jenni had called him. He'd prayed. He'd searched the Scripture. He'd become angry, and he'd wept. But he'd never stopped loving her.

He pulled his car into her driveway with Lady prancing back and forth across the backseat. Jenni had suggested he bring her for Cory. He turned off the ignition, and before he could open the door, Cory flew from the house with his arms open.

"Todd," he called. "I missed you!"

Todd stepped to the ground and enclosed the boy in his arms. "I missed you, too, pal."

Lady leaped over the front seat and wriggled her way into their circle.

Cory laughed as the dog licked his cheek. Then he dug into his pocket and pulled out the Petoskey

Stone. "Aunt Jenni let me have this. I told her you promised to give me one."

"She did?" He smiled, but seeing Cory with the stone made him uneasy. He'd asked Jenni to keep it to remember his promise.

With the boy clinging to his side and Lady tangling around his ankles, Todd made his way up the porch steps. When he reached the top, Jenni stood in the doorway. A tender smile curved her lips.

"Thank you for coming," she said, pushing the door open. She sounded reserved and nervous.

He stepped inside, longing to kiss her, but not certain he should. "I see you gave Cory the stone."

"He bugged me to death. It's on loan, although to him, it's forever."

"A loan," he said, his heart lifting at his foolish fears.

Cory and Lady charged through the living room and wrestled on the carpet.

"Why don't you play outside, Cory? You can't roughhouse in here."

Cory gave her a sour look but hoisted himself up and headed toward the back door with Lady bounding behind him.

Todd grinned, understanding her motive to bring along the dog. "Peace and quiet."

"Privacy," she said, walking toward him. She grasped a covered bowl and extended it to him. "Would you like a kiss?"

Her coy look made him smile, remembering when they first met. He shook his head. "No, but I'd love the real thing."

Jenni set the candy on the table, then returned to his side and stood so close he could smell the scent of her shampoo. She lifted her arms and entwined them around his neck as her lips found his, her mouth sweet and warm as melted chocolate.

Todd felt her tremble, and he clung to her, feeling the love he'd kept bottled up for the past week spread its warmth through his heart.

"I love you," Jenni whispered. "I'm sorry. Forgive me."

He let his kiss answer. Her hand slid up his neck, and he felt her fingers playing in his hair. While his pulse soared, he drew her closer, knowing marriage united two people as one. Today his heart joined hers, like two candles melting together, with the warmth of their love.

When their lips parted, Todd kissed her eyelids and the tip of her nose, then pressed his cheek against her head and whispered into her hair, "I've prayed so hard for this, Jenni. You wouldn't answer my calls and avoided me at the store. I didn't know what to think."

"Think I was a coward. Think I almost let go of God's special gift for me."

He tilted her chin upward and looked into her eyes. "All I can think is that God is good."

She gave him a slow nod. "After you'd left, I felt such despair and loneliness. I read the book of Job, feeling as abandoned by God as I felt when my father turned his back. Yet I prayed. I kept asking the Lord for courage to keep you out of my life. Do you know what the Lord said to me?"

Todd shook his head.

"God sent some verses from Job into my head. 'Submit to God and be at peace with Him; in this way prosperity will come to you. Accept instruction from His mouth and lay up His words in your heart.' Those words settled over me like cool water on a feverish forehead, and the meaning struck me."

"We've both fought submission, Jenni."

"I know, and the answer was so easy." She raised her hand and rested it on his cheek. "God's promise is faithful. I thought of your promise, my secret dream that I'd be swept away despite my disfigurement. The Bible says, 'You have granted him the desire of his heart and have not withheld the request of his lips.' You are the desire of my heart, Todd Bronski."

"And you're mine, Jenni Anderson." He drank in her beauty. No earthly flaw could dissuade him from the inner beauty he'd found in her. Todd drew in a breath, praying again that he would hear the answer he so longed for. "Will you marry me, Jenni?"

"Todd, be patient with me. I love you, but I need your support."

"I will," he said, holding his breath as he waited for her answer.

"Yes, I'll marry you. Yes, from the bottom of my heart."

Todd's lips met hers again, so filled with love and joy, truly the most loving kiss he'd ever known.

Chapter Seventeen

The following June

A gentle breeze drifted from Lake Michigan and ruffled the lace skirt of Jenni's wedding gown. The warm sun could not equal the fire in her heart for the man and child who stood beside her in the sand, their bare feet sinking into the blanketing white crystals.

Behind her sat their friends from Fellowship Church and Unity Church, people from town and, best of all, her father and Margaret. Her father's oxygen tank was propped beside him, but despite the inconvenience, he had come to share this precious day.

She couldn't forget Cory's face nor her father's when the two met. The occasion brought tears to her eyes, and she thanked God for giving her the courage to ask forgiveness. Today she had asked again. Moments ago she'd repeated the pastor's words to love and honor and respect Todd to the end of her days. She'd promised to be a wife, all the way, not holding back her body or her love. Now the worry about her scars sank into her thoughts. She feared seeing Todd's face when the reality struck him.

Yet as the thought nearly drowned her in fear, God's promise touched her like a life preserver on a stormy sea. She recalled when Jesus rebuked the waves and calmed the storm. "Where is your faith?" He'd asked.

Where was her faith? She lifted her head to the warming sun, wrapped in the sureness that Todd was at her side, her hand in his, wedding rings symbolizing their union.

The pastor's voice rose over the sound of the surf. "May the almighty God, Father, Son and Holy Spirit, keep you in His light and truth and love now and forever. Amen." He smiled. "You may kiss your bride."

Jenni looked into Todd's glowing eyes before hers closed with the touch of his wind-cooled lips against hers, but warmth filled her heart.

When they parted, Todd's eyes were filled with emotion. "I love you now and forever," he whispered.

"Ladies and gentlemen, let me present Mr. and Mrs. Todd Bronski."

The well-wishers rose and applauded as Todd

stepped forward to lead Jenni down the aisle, but before he moved, Cory's excited voice stopped them—Cory, her newly adopted son.

"Look," he said, clutching something in his hand. "I found it in the sand."

"What is it?" Jenni asked, forgetting her waiting guests to see what had thrilled him so much.

Todd's chuckle met her ears and his arm slipped around her waist. "God's sent us his blessing." He pointed to the object in Cory's hand.

Jenni lowered her gaze from Cory's beaming face to his palm. There lay a large smooth Petoskey Stone. She lifted her eyes heavenward, knowing God had sent them their very own sunbeam of promise.

Jenni stood behind the bathroom door, goose-flesh prickling her skin. She slipped her wedding dress onto a hanger, then hung it on the bathroom hook. The dress had been perfect, a tea-length gown adorned with seed pearls and iridescent beads.

The images of the afternoon filled her mind. Todd looked so handsome in his dark suit, and they'd laughed when he'd rolled up his pant legs as his feet slipped deeper into the sand.

He'd been so thoughtful, thinking of every detail that her addled mind had missed. His friend Dale and Dale's new wife, Bev, had invited Cory to spend the night. Cory, and Bev's son, Michael, had hit it off the day they met.

But now she waited behind the door, feeling the sleek satin of her pale blue nightgown brush against her skin. She knew Todd was patiently waiting for her. He understood.

She slipped on the matching robe and tied it, the soft fabric caressed her feet as she stepped back to unlock the door, just as she needed to unlock her fear. She placed her hand on the doorknob, praying Todd's face wouldn't reflect his disgust when he saw her scars, but praying she would understand if he did.

A voice echoed in her thoughts. "Why are you troubled, and why do doubts rise in your minds? Look at My hands and My feet. It is I Myself! Touch Me and see." Her mind filled with the vision of Jesus, innocent, yet wounded and afflicted for her sins. Why did she weep for her small loss compared to the Lord's saving sacrifice?

Jenni turned the knob and drew in a lengthy breath, then pulled open the door.

Todd's head pivoted as she stepped into the room. He rose and walked toward her, his gaze riveted to hers, then slowly glided over her full length. "You look beautiful."

"So do you," she said, gazing at his broad chest beneath his white T-shirt.

He drew her into his arms, resting his cheek on her hair and holding her close. She trembled beside him, wondering and waiting, for what she'd feared for so many years.

Moments passed before he released her with a gentle caress and slid his hand into hers, then led her across the room. Jenni's heart swelled as he dimmed the lights to a soft glow, then untied her robe and slipped it from her shoulders.

She stood before him, draped in the satin gown that hid her sorrow. Jenni waited breathlessly, her heart thundering against her chest.

Todd lowered his face and kissed her neck and shoulder. Her knees trembled in a muddle of longing and dread. He touched her cheek, and her eyes shifted to his, his question evident in the tender look.

Jenni moved past him and sat on the edge of the bed, slipping her feet beneath the cool sheets. Todd sat beside her, his loving gaze holding her captive. "I love you, Jenni Bronski. You've given me a gift today. You and Cory. I'm the happiest man alive."

"I'm honored and blessed to be your wife." Though hushed, her words were sure.

He sought her gaze again, asking permission without words. She answered with her eyes.

Gently Todd moved his hand to one shoulder and drew down the slender strap of her gown. She couldn't look, afraid what she'd see on his face.

A warm tear struck her skin as Todd bent to kiss her scar. When his gaze met hers, tears rimmed his eyes. "Thank you," he whispered, his finger brushing her wound. "Thank you for trusting me."

The tenderness in his voice lifted Jenni's heart and spirit. "Thank you for loving me."

"You have not disappointed me, Jenni. You are still the most beautiful woman in the world."

With the Lord, all things are possible. The thought warmed her as Todd's kisses took her the first step on their journey together.

* * * * *

And now, turn the page
for a sneak preview of
Windigo Twilight,
the first book in the
GREAT LAKES LEGENDS miniseries
by Colleen Rhoads,
part of Steeple Hill's exciting new line,
Love Inspired Suspense!

On sale in August 2005
from Steeple Hill books.

Prologue

The sun threw a last golden glow across the horizon of Lake Superior. From her vantage point about five miles from Eagle Island, Suzanne Baxter could see nothing but the cold, clear waters of the big lake they call Gitchee Gumee.

She leaned against the railing of the forty-foot yacht and lifted her face to the breeze. Her husband, Mason, joined her.

"I'm glad we came," she said, turning to slip her arms around his still-trim body. Even at fifty-four, he could still make her heart race like a teenager's. They'd come through so much over the years.

He dropped a kiss on top of her head. "Me, too. It was time to make amends."

She bristled. "You mean let them make amends. *You* didn't do anything."

"Don't start," he said. "It was the right thing to do."

"I'm not so sure anyone but your mother feels that way. The rest stand to lose a lot of money with you back in your mother's good graces. She intends to leave you the lion's share now as her only living child." She pulled away and rubbed her arms.

"They'll get used to it." He swept his hand over the railing. "I can't believe we allowed ourselves to be gone from this for fifteen years. The kids should have been here every summer."

"We'll all come out in August. Jake will be done with his dig by mid-July, and Wynne's dive should be over about the same time. Becca will be out of school. I miss them."

"We'll be home by Wednesday. You could call Becca on the ship-to-shore phone. She should be around."

Suzanne hesitated. She'd like nothing better than to share things with her youngest child, but something still didn't feel right about the situation. She'd caught undercurrents at the old manor house, eddies of danger she wasn't about to share with her daughter yet. Becca would just worry. "I'll see her in a few days," she said.

He nodded and pulled her back against his chest as they watched the sun plunging into the water.

A rumble started under her feet, a vibration that made her toes feel tingly. It radiated up her calves. "What is that?" she asked Mason.

He frowned. His hand began to slide from her

waist as he turned to check it out. But the rumble became a roar as the hull of the boat burst apart. The explosion tossed Suzanne into the air. As she hurtled toward the frigid Lake Superior water, her last regretful thought was of her children.

Chapter One

"I applied for a job on the island." Waiting for a response from her siblings on the three-way conference call, Rebecca Baxter gripped her cordless phone until her fingers cramped. No telling how loud the opposition would be, though it was in her favor that her brother was in Montserrat and her sister in Argentina.

The answering hum in the line made her wonder if the conference call with her siblings had gotten disconnected. Then she heard Jake's long sigh and braced herself for his reaction.

"You're not going anywhere. The estate isn't settled yet, and you promised to do it," Jake said.

Her brother's reaction was surprisingly mild, but after twenty-five years, Becca knew he was the maddest when he was the quietest.

"I had a phone interview this afternoon, and it

went great. Not many people know about Ojibwa culture and not many would be willing to go to a deserted island in the middle of Lake Superior. I'm pretty sure I'll get the job." Her voice didn't even tremble, and she gave herself a thumbs-up of approval. She couldn't let them know how terrified she really was. This was the new Becca—strong and courageous.

"Jake, settle down." Her sister Wynne's soft voice was mellow enough to tame him. As head of an archaeological team, Jake sometimes forgot his sisters didn't have to jump at his command, not even Becca, the youngest.

"Don't encourage her!" This time there was no doubt about his displeasure.

Becca winced and held the phone out from her ear for a moment then put it back. "You can't stop me, Jake. Max Duncan seemed very impressed with my credentials." Even if he sounded as gruff as a grizzly bear. She grimaced and waited for the next objection.

"That was cousin Laura's husband, right?" Wynne asked. "He's still there even though she's dead?"

"Yep. He's a writer. I found out he was researching a new novel set on an Ojibwa reservation and offered my expertise."

Jake snorted. "A perfect job for a career student like you. You've done some harebrained things in the past, but we're both too far away to bail you out of trouble this time."

"Jake," Wynne warned again.

"Okay, she just caught me off guard." His voice softened. "You seem so certain the explosion wasn't an accident. I'm not so sure, Becca. You don't have a shred of evidence."

Defensive hackles raised along Becca's back. Jake was a man of science who would scoff at the way she felt things. "I know it in my heart," she said quietly. "I'm not going to let them get away with it."

"I think it's just the way you're dealing with Mom and Dad's deaths. No one rigged the boat to blow. It was an accident."

Becca thought her brother's emphatic announcement was his way of convincing himself, but she kept that opinion to herself.

"Gram will recognize you," Wynne said.

It was Becca's main fear. "I applied as Becca Lynn and left off my last name altogether. I was ten the last time I saw her, and everyone was still calling me Becky. Besides, Max mentioned she was away on a trip to Europe. I've got four weeks to find out who killed them."

"Max and Laura had a little girl, didn't they?" Wynne's voice was thoughtful.

"Molly. She's five. She would have been only two when Laura died."

"There was some question that maybe Max had

killed her, wasn't there? I don't like this, Becca." Wynne sounded worried.

Becca could picture her older sister clearly. She missed Wynne with a sudden pang. The funeral a month ago had been a kaleidoscope of pain and disbelief where mourners and family moved through the landscape in a blur of pats and hugs. There had been no real time to grieve together.

No one from the island had come. The thought made her press her lips together and scowl. Gram had outlived all three sons. The least Gram could have done was bid her last son farewell.

The lump in her throat grew until she wasn't sure she could speak. Becca sipped her licorice tea, cold now with a gray scum on top. The call waiting beeped, and she glanced at it. "I have to go. Max is calling me back. I'll let you know when I get to Windigo Manor."

She clicked the button and answered the new call. "Becca Lynn."

"When can you come?" Max Duncan's deep voice asked.

"Immediately," she answered.

As she made arrangements to be picked up at the boat dock, she wondered what she was getting herself in for. But she had to try.

Dear Reader,

Every story I write speaks to you of God's gracious love and mercy. This one is no different. I also wanted to share a story with you that would tease chocolate lovers' taste buds as well as leave you with a thoughtful message. Breast cancer is a beatable disease if you would take the time for self-checks and mammograms.

Jenni had to deal with the difficulty of breast cancer at an early age and nearly allowed it to destroy her life until she was able to give her burden to the Lord and to trust Todd's promise that he loved her for who she was inside. How often we carry our burdens and lack faith that God can make all things work for the good of those who love Him.

Please keep that thought in your heart, and for a special treat, here's the recipe for Todd's accidental bark or, as he called it, Chocolate Surprise. Melt one pound of white or dark chocolate wafers in a double boiler. When melted thoroughly, add one cup of broken pretzel sticks, one cup nuts (peanuts, Spanish nuts or almonds), and for variety, add one cup dried cherries or cranberries. Mix quickly and pour onto a cookie sheet covered with waxed paper. Spread into a thin layer and put in the freezer until firm. When it's ready, break it into pieces and enjoy.

I wish you a lifetime of good health and happiness, and, as always, I pray God sends you His richest blessings.

Gail Gaymer Martin